Olivia
and the
Great Escape

LYN GARDNER

nosy
crow

First published in the UK in 2013 by Nosy Crow Ltd
The Crow's Nest, 10a Lant Street
London, SE1 1QR, UK

Nosy Crow and associated logos are trademarks and/or registered
trademarks of Nosy Crow Ltd

Text copyright © Lyn Gardner, 2013

Printed and bound in the UK by Clays Ltd, St. Ives Plc
Typeset by Tiger Media Ltd, Bishops Stortford, Hertfordshire

Papers used by Nosy Crow are made from wood grown in
sustainable forests

ISBN: 978 0 85763 152 7

www.nosycrow.com

Chapter One

Olivia, Tom and Eel raced up the steps of the Swan Academy of Theatre and Dance and into the entrance hall. Georgia was standing by the staircase looking anxious, with Aeysha and Katie by her side. A number of Swans were milling around, greeting each other delightedly and showering each other with hugs to show how pleased they were to be back at school at the start of a new term. Eel pushed her way on through the crowd to where her friend, Emmy, was standing.

"Where have you two been?" demanded Georgia of Olivia and Tom. "And why haven't you been answering your phones?"

Aeysha grinned. "Georgia's a bit het up. I told her you'd both decided to run away and join a circus. I said you weren't coming back this term and were chucking in the Swan forever."

"Never!" said Olivia and Tom in unison, which made everyone laugh.

"I'm not *that* gullible," said Georgia, so crossly that it made everyone laugh again.

"Sorry, Georgie," said Tom as he felt in his pocket. "I didn't realise my phone was off. But we're here now, and assembly hasn't started yet so we haven't missed anything important, have we?"

Georgia shook her head.

"It'll start any minute now, though," said Katie. "Lots of people are in the hall already."

"But where have you both been? I can tell from the look on your faces that you've got a secret," persisted Georgia. "Come on, spill."

Tom glanced at Olivia, who shook her head. "Sorry, Georgie," he said. "It's got to stay a secret for a while yet."

Georgia looked put out. "But we're your friends, you can trust us," she said. "You know we'd never give any of your secrets away."

"Oh, Georgia, of course we know that," said Olivia. "I'd trust you all with my life!" But it was clear from the hurt look on Georgia's face that she wasn't placated. "Listen, Georgie, it's not even certain that what we can't tell you about is even going to happen. When I know that it is, I promise that you, Aeysha and Katie will be the very first to know."

"Just my luck that I'll be off in Yorkshire filming when something exciting is about to happen," said Katie.

"But that's really thrilling too, Katie," said Olivia. "We're all really made up for you. You so deserve to have got that TV series."

The others nodded enthusiastically as the first bell for assembly rang loudly. Olivia could see her grandmother, Alicia Swan, slowly making her way down the stairs on her way to the assembly hall.

As they turned to go in, Olivia noticed a boy she had never seen before slouched against the far wall, watching them. He saw her glancing his way, and very coolly raised an eyebrow and gave her a casual salute. An amused smile played around his lips.

"Who's that?" hissed Georgia as they crowded into the hall.

Olivia shrugged. "Never seen him before in my life."

"He must be new," said Aeysha. "Bit full of himself, isn't he? Most people are pretty nervous on their first day at the Swan."

"Anyone who looks like that probably has every reason to be mega confident," said Katie.

"Well, I suppose he is very good-looking," said Aeysha, a little grudgingly.

"Good-looking? He's drop-dead gorgeous," breathed Georgia. Then she added dreamily, "I hope he's in our class." Then she realised everyone was staring at her and blushed like mad and wished she hadn't said anything.

"Oh, Georgie girl, I always thought you only had eyes for me. I'm crushed," said Tom. "My heart is shattered into a thousand tiny shards." He swooned dramatically, making the others laugh and giving Georgia a chance to recover herself.

"Don't worry, Tom, I'll lend you my superglue to stick it back together," said Olivia, just as her phone rang. She answered it hurriedly, aware that the school prefects were giving her the evil eye.

"Hey, I'm in assembly so it's got to be quick. Any news?" She listened and then squealed. The prefects tutted loudly. Aeysha, Georgia and

Katie looked at each other surprised. Olivia was not a squealer even when she was really excited. But her cheeks were flushed and her eyes were shining. "OK gotta go, thanks for telling me." Olivia looked wildly around and spotted Eel standing with Emmy in a gaggle of her classmates just ahead of them.

"Eel! Eel!" Eel swung around at her sister's voice. "It's on, Eel! It's on!" Olivia cried just as the hall was beginning to quieten. Tom gave a low whoop but Eel let out a great shout of excitement and high-fived her sister, making everyone turn and stare at her and Olivia.

"What is it? What's on?" hissed Georgia urgently. "Tell us!"

But at that moment Alicia's crisp tones cut through the noise. "Olivia. Eel. If you've quite finished, perhaps assembly can begin." But even their grandmother's reprimand couldn't stop Eel jiggling from foot to foot or the grin spreading across Olivia's face.

"After," she whispered to her friends out of the corner of her mouth. "I'll tell you all straight after. I promise."

Alicia Swan looked around the hall at her

pupils. She loved the start of the new school term. Whenever she thought that she had failed her Swans – which was almost every day – she comforted herself with the thought of how eager they all were to return to the school after every holiday. Many of them had their difficulties, but so many blossomed at the Swan.

She had been delighted to see Katie Wilkes-Cox and Kylie Morris chatting away to each other, and she was thrilled by the progress of both her granddaughters. Olivia had such a strong, loyal circle of friends, and Eel was a cheeky little devil loved by pupils and staff alike. Eel's dancing was quite extraordinary for somebody just nine years old, particularly as she had started taking lessons so recently. Alicia felt honoured to be getting a chance to nurture such a talent but she was also aware of so much that could go wrong: injury, illness, a sudden growth spurt that could out-fox even the most gifted.

She glanced towards the new boy, Alex Parks, who had sauntered in at the last minute and was leaning against the wall at the back of the hall looking around as if he was enjoying some private joke. At his audition he had demonstrated undoubted acting talent and he had a good strong singing voice, which was why she'd offered him a place at the Swan. He was certainly good-looking enough to have a shot at modelling. There was a charisma about him, too. She could see some of the Year Nine and Ten girls nudging each other and giggling. She just hoped he wasn't going to be trouble. She had a feeling he probably liked to play the bad boy. If that was the case, she didn't want any of her hard-working Swans distracted by him.

Alicia cleared her throat. "Good afternoon, Swans," she began. "It's lovely to see you all back here for another term. We've an addition to the school this term: Alex Parks will be joining Year Nine and will be taking the acting and musical-theatre strands." She nodded towards Alex. "I'm sure you'll all make him very welcome."

Kylie grinned and whispered to Katie. "I reckon Georgia's not the only one who'd like to make him feel welcome."

Katie shrugged. "Maybe, but I reckon Aeysha's right. There's something arrogant behind that pretty face. Anyway, I don't suppose he'll give any of us a second look."

Alicia was continuing to speak. "As you

know, a number of Swans are already playing the West End or filming this term, and Katie Wilkes-Cox and Sara Asgard are our latest successes. They will both be going to Yorkshire for a month a little later in the term to film a new TV series, *Orphan Girls*, which is set in an Edwardian orphanage." Olivia and the others grinned at Katie as they joined in the cheers.

"As usual," continued Alicia, "all job opportunities and upcoming auditions will be posted on the notice board near my office. Year Nine will be staging *A Midsummer Night's Dream* at the beautiful Campion's music hall just down the road for parents and friends at the end of term. I'm sure it's going to be lovely. I've seen some of the drawings for costume designs, which Lily Carmichael has done, and they are very elegant. A mixture of modern, Edwardian and 1930s chic. The idea is to create something timeless. Sebastian Shaw, who is directing, has decided to set the play in a garden with a bower and garlanded swings. I think it will be quite magical.

"There will also be a junior evening of choral work." Alicia smiled at the juniors. "I am very much looking forward to hearing Year

Three's staged version of TS Eliot's *Macavity the Mystery Cat* as it's one of my favourite poems.

"Now, those of you in the school who are keen singer-songwriters may be interested in this: there is a nationwide competition taking place to find the country's best songwriters under the age of eighteen. An impressive array of judges from the industry has been lined up. Anyone who is interested should come and see me and I'll give you the details. It would be good to have some Swan entrants. You can enter singly, in pairs or in groups. Collaborators are allowed as long as they are under eighteen. If there's enough interest, old boy Kasha Kasparian has offered to come in and give a couple of workshops to help you develop your ideas. Kasha, as I'm sure you know, recently signed to Dumbfounded Records."

There was a buzz of excitement. Kasha had only left the Swan last summer, but at seventeen he had already had a number one hit, was busy at work on an album and had some gig dates later in the term that had sold out almost as soon as they'd been announced. Everywhere he went he was followed by screaming teenage girls.

Alicia looked at her watch. "I hope this is going to be a very happy and productive term for all of you. Now, to your first lessons, please."

Everyone was turning to leave when Alicia called: "Olivia! Tom! Can you and your friends take Alex to acting class with you? Help him out for a few days while he finds his feet and his way around, would you? The Swan is such a warren, he may need a bit of looking after."

Olivia and the others nodded, and Alex swaggered lazily towards them. Georgia gave him a big welcoming smile.

"Hmm," muttered Aeysha to Katie. "I'm not sure he needs our help. I reckon that Alex Parks won't have the slightest difficulty in looking after himself."

Chapter Two

Olivia and the others pushed their way through the throng of children towards the Ashcroft studio where they would be having their first acting lesson of the term with Sebastian Shaw. They had been told to prepare a speech from *A Midsummer Night's Dream* so they knew the class was also an informal audition.

But Olivia's mind wasn't on the play. Her brain was busy processing the news that she'd had by phone just before assembly began. Now it was confirmed, she was bursting to tell her friends. She didn't think she could bear to sit through acting class without sharing it with them, although she would have to swear them all to secrecy. But she also knew she couldn't say anything while Alex was around.

She was suddenly aware of him at her side, and that he had asked her a question that she hadn't heard. She felt embarrassed.

"I'm so sorry Alex, I wasn't listening properly. What did you say?" she asked, with a luminous but distracted smile.

"Olivia, you never listen!" said Georgia, shaking her head and raising her eyebrows as if she were dealing with a difficult toddler. "Alex was asking about the Swan panto last year. I was telling him how much fun it was."

"Let me guess," said Alex, giving Olivia an intense, moody stare. "You played the beautiful princess."

Georgia looked put out, and Tom raised an eyebrow just a fraction. Olivia gave a great peal of laughter that sounded just like a lovely bell.

"Goodness no," said Olivia. "I was the back end of the pantomime horse. It was mint. Georgie was Cinderella. She was dazzling."

Georgia looked pleased and suitably bashful as they trooped into the Ashcroft studio. Kylie and Connor were already there, putting out the chairs.

"Alex, you can put your things down

there," said Olivia, pointing him towards the corner. "Kylie, Con, could you look after Alex a moment? There's something the others and I have got to do quickly. By ourselves." She gave him an apologetic little smile. "Sorry, Alex. It's just that it's private."

Alex put his hands up. "Don't mind me," he said, looking directly at Olivia. "Be as mysterious as you like. It's always so alluring." Olivia wasn't really listening, but Tom looked irritated and Aeysha seemed to be struggling not to laugh.

"I'd be more than happy to look after him," said Kylie, looking pleased. She flashed Georgia a little smile of triumph as she walked towards Alex.

"Come on, quick!" said Olivia to the others. She beckoned them out of the studio and into the corridor where it was quiet. Georgia looked back towards Alex a little wistfully. She didn't want Kylie getting too friendly with the new boy.

"Georgia! Are you listening?" asked Olivia, brusquely.

Georgia bristled at her tone. "Of course I am!" she snapped. "I just think you were really rude to Alex. You've hardly listened to a word he's said to you and then you just dumped him on Kylie, even though we were the ones Miss Swan asked to look after him!"

Katie and Aeysha exchanged a glance.

"Sorry, Georgia," said Olivia, looking surprised. "But this news isn't for sharing with strangers, and I thought you were dying to hear it."

"I was, I mean I am," said Georgia, still glancing back towards the studio.

"OK, I'm going to let you all into a big secret, but you've got to promise not to tell until it's announced in a couple of weeks. If it gets out and I'm to blame, I'd die of shame."

Everyone nodded vigorously.

"Of course we won't tell," said Georgia a little shortly. "Cross our hearts."

Olivia grinned excitedly. "Dad's doing another stunt. Down by Tower Bridge. That's where Tom and Eel and I were this morning. We went to see the site. He's there now with Pablo making preparations. It's taken months to get permission. At one point, he thought he'd never get it because a Russian guy called Viktor wanted to do something similar, and it's been touch and go which one would get the go-ahead. This Viktor guy is pretty young and inexperienced. He's done some stunts in Eastern Europe but he's virtually unknown here and hasn't done all that much high-wire. What he has got, though, is a hot-shot manager behind him, a guy called Ethan Rees, who Pablo says always gets the deals he wants. But not this time!"

"What's Jack actually going to do?" asked Katie excitedly. "I mean, he's already walked across Tower Bridge on the high-wire."

"It's much more thrilling than that," said Olivia, her eyes shining. She paused dramatically and whispered: "He's going to live on a high wire stretched across the Thames for thirty days and nights. Sleep there, too, right on the wire. Whatever the weather. Nobody's ever done anything like it before. If he succeeds, it will be a world record."

"But that's insane!" cried Katie.

"That's what Gran thinks, too."

"And she may be right," said Tom. "It's certainly going to be a challenge. I just hope he's got good waterproofs."

"If anyone can do it, it's Jack," said Olivia firmly. "But not a word to anybody. We don't want to spoil the announcement when it's made in a few weeks' time. Promise?"

"We promise," chorused her friends. Olivia smiled. She knew she could trust them not to tell a soul.

Just then, Sebastian Shaw, the acting teacher, poked his head out of the door and enquired dryly, "Do you lot intend to grace us with your presence, or don't you want parts in the show?"

"Sorry, Mr Shaw," they chorused as they walked back into the room. Olivia slipped into the nearest empty seat that, much to Georgia's annoyance, just happened to be next to Alex. Georgia plonked herself down grumpily into a seat in the row behind.

Alex turned to Olivia as she sat down and whispered something to her. Then he casually put his arm along the back of her chair, taking care not to actually touch her, but as if he were staking some kind of claim. Olivia was completely oblivious to what was going on, and to the fact that Georgia was looking daggers at her. But Tom, Katie and Aeysha didn't miss a single thing.

Chapter Three

Eel was standing in Alicia's office, hopping from foot to foot. Alicia and the ballet teacher, India Taylor, were both sitting on the red velvet sofa with its paisley throw that gave the entire room a dramatic look, like the set for a play.

"I just want to know," said Eel, so passionately that she made Alicia and India smile, "I just want to know if I'm good enough. I don't see why it's such a problem to tell me. I just want the truth. If I'm not good enough, I'd prefer to know, and if I am it would be useful to know so I can plan accordingly."

Alicia's mouth twitched at Eel's last words, which made her nine-year-old granddaughter sound like a middle-aged manager at a sales conference. She never stopped marvelling at

Eel, who always seemed so old beyond her years and who, unlike her elder sister, Olivia, had a triple helping of self-confidence.

"Eel, dear," said Alicia, "I've told you before. Nobody can predict how talent will develop. Over the years we've had some remarkable dancers pass through the Swan, but an early blossoming talent doesn't always come to fruition or ensure future success."

"Your grandmother's right," said India Taylor. She spoke directly to Alicia. "Remember Jessie Milan? A wonderful ballet dancer. She went on to the Imperial School but then she got injured and the injury recurred and in the end she had to give up. Then there was Gina Constable. We thought she was a dead cert for either the Imperial or the Royal Ballet School, but both of them said she'd grow too tall, and they were right. She became a lawyer. Specialises in showbiz clients. She's very successful, I hear."

"But," insisted Eel, "you knew that those girls had a real talent. All I want to know is whether I do, too. I know I'm good, I just want you to tell me if I'm good enough. I don't think it's unreasonable to ask."

"Eel, darling," said Alicia. "You've got to

realise that most girls here started ballet when they were four or five, sometimes even younger. You've only been dancing a year. Your progress has been phenomenal. But what we don't know is whether you will continue to progress at the same rate."

"You mean I may have already peaked?" asked Eel, gloomily.

"Possible, but not probable," said India. "Not in my experience."

Alicia smiled patiently at her grand-daughter. "Listen, Eel, the Swan is a hot-bed of talent. Just to get through the doors, pupils have to be immensely talented and immensely dedicated. But did I know when an eleven-year-old Theo Deacon arrived here that he'd go on to be Hollywood's highest paid movie star? When I had to coax Kasha Kasparian out of a cupboard when he was seven because he was so scared of performing, did I know that almost ten years later he'd be an international pop star being chased down the road by screaming girls? Of course not, because it wasn't just the fact that they were talented that got them where they are now, there were other factors too, including hard work and a great big dollop of luck."

"I know all that," said Eel impatiently. "I know that you can't tell me if I'll have the same luck or whether I'll get run over by a bus next week and never dance again, but I don't see why you can't tell me if you think I might have what it takes to be a ballerina."

"Because we don't know yet what the depth and breadth of your talent is, Eel," said Alicia. "Talent reveals itself in mysterious ways."

Eel sighed loudly. "Well, if you can't tell me, I'll just have to find out for myself then."

She left the room, banging the door behind her. Alicia and India looked at each other.

"She's extraordinary," said India. "She's very single-minded and prepared to work unbelievably hard. Combine that with a mighty talent and I reckon she could do anything she wanted."

"Tell me truthfully, India, she is as good as I think, isn't she?" Alicia looked worried. "I'd hate to think that I was letting my love for her cloud my judgment. You would tell me if I were?"

India Taylor smiled. "No worries on that score, Alicia. She is a genuine ballet talent. Like you, I believe she has the talent to make it to the very top, but as you told her yourself, there are plenty of other factors that come into it. And of course others may not agree. Remember Chloe Hertz? We all really rated her and she was devastated when neither the Imperial nor the Royal Ballet School took her. She never really recovered from the blow."

"That was a real lesson in not piling too many expectations upon a child or getting up the parents' hopes," said Alicia. "Excessive enthusiasm about a child's prospects can be very damaging."

"Yes, that's true," said India, "but I do wonder whether your Eel may be the exception. Maybe children like her do need to know early the extent of their gift, and are tough and flexible enough to deal with the truth and may actually benefit from knowing." India paused. "Of course, there is a way, not surefire I know, but it would give a pretty good indication. Put her up to audition for the Imperial this term. I know you've always thought it was better to wait until our pupils can try out for both the Imperial and the Royal Ballet School at the time of secondary school transfer, but maybe in this instance…"

"And if she got in?" asked Alicia quietly.

"Ah," said India sagely, "then you'd have to deal with losing her."

After India Taylor left, Alicia sat thinking for a long while. She hoped her motives in not raising Eel's expectations about her future were the right ones. But maybe India was right and Eel *was* different from other children. She was certainly way more independent and confident than most children her age. Her upbringing in a travelling circus had ensured that. Maybe she did need to know the true extent of her talent?

But if Eel got a place at the Imperial, Alicia wasn't sure she could bear losing the granddaughter who she had only found a little more than a year ago. She sighed. She would have to talk to Jack and between them decide what they thought was in Eel's best interests. She just hoped that what they thought was in Eel's best interests, and what Eel thought was in Eel's best interests, turned out to be one and the same.

Chapter Four

Tom turned as the door of the little rehearsal studio at the top of the school opened and Georgia, Aeysha, Katie and Alex appeared. He quickly put his finger to his lips to tell them to keep quiet. Olivia was on the wire and she was so intent on what she was doing that she hadn't even heard the door open, or noticed the others arrive. She was balancing on the wire on top of two chairs that were wedged one upside down on top of the other so they fitted together like the pieces of a 3D jigsaw. For a moment the structure she had made wobbled, and it looked as if she and the chairs would collapse and fall, but Olivia adjusted her weight and miraculously the structure stayed upright. The others held their breath. They could see the muscles in her arms twitch and her forehead was frowned in concentration. She held the pose for a count of five and then nodded at Tom who ran forward to grab the chairs as Olivia let go of them and jumped off the wire. Everyone broke into spontaneous applause.

"Wow," said Alex. "That was amazing. Did you learn to do it here?"

Olivia shook her head. "My sister and I lived in a circus. It was our dad's: the Great Marvello's Circus of Wonders. We toured all over Europe, and to Ireland and Scotland."

Alex looked impressed. "So your dad must be the Jack Marvell who does all those extreme high-wire stunts? I've seen loads on YouTube."

Olivia nodded proudly. "The one and only."

"I'd love to have a dad like that. Is he working on anything now?" asked Alex curiously.

"Oh, he's doing—" began Georgia excitedly, and then stopped abruptly and put a hand over her mouth as she realised what she was saying. She turned bright red and Olivia glared at her.

"He's always working on something," said

24

Aeysha smoothly. "Isn't he, Livy?"

Olivia nodded. "And sometimes he teaches high-wire here."

"Yes," said Tom, "so if you wanted to learn..."

"That would be cool." Alex looked right into Olivia's eyes and said lazily, "But I'd prefer you to teach me."

Olivia didn't seem to notice the intensity of his manner, but Aeysha and Katie looked at each other and made a face. Georgia frowned as if she was a bit miffed, and Tom said a little too quickly: "I don't think Liv would have time."

Olivia shook her head. "Tom's right. I wouldn't. It's a real struggle to find time for Tom and I to practise together."

"So you walk the wire, too?" asked Alex, turning to Tom and looking him up and down as if assessing him in some way.

"Yep," said Tom, and then he added perhaps a little too gleefully: "Liv taught me."

"Yes," said Aeysha loyally, "and Tom is a complete natural."

"He's very good," said Olivia, with such pride in her voice that Tom actually felt his heart swell. Olivia wasn't one for gushing praise.

She had once made him practice the same notoriously tricky move on the wire for over an hour without a break, and when he eventually got it right she had simply said that he was coming along quite nicely – for a beginner.

"I did a bit of tightrope walking when I was younger," said Alex. "I used to go to a circus-skills workshop on Saturdays when I was a kid. I was quite good at it actually, so I could probably be again."

"I bet you could," said Georgia. "Why don't you show us what you can do?"

"OK," said Alex and he jumped on to the wire. He took a few steps and promptly fell off again.

"Bad luck," said Georgia.

"Must be a bit out of practice," the boy said, his supreme confidence seemingly undentable.

"Here," said Olivia, getting a stick. "Get back on and try with your finger tips touching this. It will just give you the security you need." She held the staff up and Alex walked along the wire supported by the stick. Alex got to the end and jumped off. He gave Olivia a dazzling smile and touched her hand.

"Thanks, Liv, that was fun. Do I show

promise?"

"Well, you're not a natural like Tom, but you'll do," said Olivia, with a brief smile. "You should join the class. But it's not for everyone. None of the other Swans have taken to the wire as well as Tom, but we've some really promising aerialists and lots of acrobats."

"Well, everyone has different skills," said Aeysha. "Livy can walk the high-wire and does trapeze, Georgia sings beautifully and just gobbles up quadratic equations, and me, I can wiggle my ears."

Everyone laughed.

"That's not true, Aeysha," said Katie. "I mean, it is true you can wiggle both your ears at the same time, I've seen you do it, and it *is* amazing, but you can do lots of brilliant things. You're a real brainiac, and you can write songs and lyrics."

"Are you going to enter the songwriting competition, Aeysh?" asked Tom.

Aeysha nodded shyly. "I thought I might have a go." She looked around. "Anyone else?"

They all shook their heads. "I couldn't write a song to save my life," said Katie.

"No," said Aeysha, "but you can do lots of

other things. You're a terrific dancer and I saw you've signed up for contortion this term. Pablo is very picky about who he lets do that."

"Ah," said Katie with a big grin. "I've been in so many tight situations in my life, he probably thought he couldn't turn me down. But I won't make much progress this term because of the filming in Yorkshire."

"What about you, Alex?" asked Tom, who was feeling a little irritated about the way Alex had called Olivia "Liv". "What's your special skill or are you just incredibly good at everything?"

Aeysha gave Tom a quick glance. It was unlike him to be snarky. But Alex didn't seem to have noticed. He looked at them all for a moment and then he opened his mouth. What came out was a complete surprise. Alex sounded just like Sebastian Shaw, and what was even more uncanny, he *looked* very like him too, even though Sebastian was at least thirty years older. The others gasped with amazement and then shrieked as before their eyes Alex morphed into Mrs Merman the jazz teacher: "Smile, children, smile. Show me your teeth."

Almost immediately he changed again and

became Alicia at the beginning of term assembly. It was so astonishing that Olivia and the others were all left open-mouthed.

"That is one of the most amazing things I've ever seen," said Aeysha, wiping away the tears of laughter. "How do you do it?"

Alex shrugged. "Think I was just born with it. My dad's got it. He used to do an impersonation act in clubs before my mum got sick. He always wanted to break into TV, but it never happened for him. He used to have a manager, this guy called Ethan, who said he'd make him the next big thing. But he didn't. But Dad hasn't given up hope. He's a much better mimic than me. I'm actually better at women than men, although that may change as I get older. He can do anyone. I'm still learning."

"Well, we're all dead impressed," said Katie.

"Even you, Liv?" asked Alex softly.

"Oh, Olivia's never impressed by anyone unless they're balancing in mid-air," said Georgia, so snitchily that the others all began talking at once to make up for her rudeness.

They didn't hear Alex say to Olivia: "Then I'll just have to sign up for high-wire classes and show you what I can do."

Chapter Five

Aeysha strummed the last note on her guitar, looked round the room and smiled. She felt tremendous relief that it had gone so well. Everyone clapped and cheered and in the very front Kasha Kasparian was clapping loudest of them all. It made Aeysha feel really proud that someone who she admired and who was a proven songwriter clearly liked her little effort.

It had been a long morning for Kasha who, at Alicia's request, had been helping the Swans start work on their compositions. Some were entering in small groups or pairs, others singly like Aeysha. He didn't really have the time but he was still so in awe of Alicia that he hadn't dreamed of saying no to her. Besides, Kasha loved being back at the Swan and had hoped that it might take his mind off other things, maybe even inspire him. The pressure to get his first album finished was intense. Particularly as he had just released a second single that showed every sign of going straight to number one.

Kasha had never realised that being a pop star was such hard work. When he had been at the Swan and immediately after he had left, the music and lyrics had just flowed out of him. He had found writing a song effortless. He had once heard a novelist say that writing a book was as easy as remembering something that hadn't happened yet, and that's what writing a song had always felt like to him.

But since his first single had gone to number one, he'd barely had a moment to himself. First there had been the Swan pantomime, *Cinderella*, which he'd loved doing but which had taken a huge amount of time, and now his life was an endless round of publicity shoots, interviews and rehearsals for his upcoming gigs. Then there was all the attention, too. He could no longer walk down Oxford Street or travel on the tube without being besieged by fans.

He didn't have time to write any new songs.

At least that's what he kept telling himself. The truth was that the inspiration seemed to have dried up. Every time he sat down at a piano or picked up his guitar, nothing came out. At first it had been frustrating, but now he was starting to feel panicky. What if he could never write another song? At least he had just enough really first class material for the album, but he had drawn on all his best old stuff to create it. If his songwriting gift had really deserted him forever, his career would be over before it had properly begun.

"That's wonderful, Aeysha, you're a real talent," said Kasha. And he meant it. Most of the songs he had heard that morning had been predictable, derivative of recent big hits including his own. But Aeysha's song, although unpolished, had a really quirky, distinctive quality that marked it out.

"I'm really impressed, Aeysha. It's genuinely promising. Maybe you could be a singer-songwriter?"

Aeysha smiled shyly. "Nah, I wouldn't want to perform. I've already decided that. It's not for me, at least not in the long term. That's why I'm leaving the Swan at the end of the year.

But I'd love to write songs for other people to sing."

"You can write one for me any time," said Kasha. "Or maybe we could write one together when I've got a bit more time? That would be fun."

"I'd really love that," said Aeysha, sincerely. The bell rang for lunch.

"I guess that's it for today," said Kasha. "We'll all meet again in a couple of weeks or so."

He walked with Aeysha down the curved staircase towards the entrance hall. "Are any of the others around? I'd love to say hello to Georgie and Livy and Tom," he said.

"Georgia will have gone to the lunchtime high-wire workshop," said Aeysha.

"Georgia? High-wire? I thought she was scared of heights?" said Kasha, frowning.

"Oh, I don't think the appeal is the high-wire itself," said Aeysha dryly. "I think the appeal is a boy."

"Lucky boy," said Kasha. "Georgia was a beautiful Cinderella."

"She was," said Aeysha, "but I'm not sure that Alex Parks is fairytale Prince material. Anyway, I think he might have his eye on someone else. Listen, you might catch Livy and Tom if they're not helping out at the workshop."

But they were nowhere to be seen, although Kasha did get to high-five Eel, who they found asking Mrs Gibbs at reception if any post had come for her dad.

Kasha said goodbye to Aeysha and walked down the steps, and as he did so his phone rang. It was Lucie Groves from his record label. Lucie was always brisk and to the point, as if the usual niceties of conversation were costing her money she felt she could ill afford. Kasha was a bit frightened of her. She had always been pleasant, even effusive towards him, but he had heard stories of acts being suddenly and mysteriously dropped when they had displeased Lucie in some way, or hadn't been as financially successful as expected. Kasha didn't think that failure was a word in Lucie's vocabulary.

"Hi Kash," she said now. "Listen, we've been talking here. We all really love the album, and I know we said it was finished, but we really think it needs one more song to balance the others. Something more down-beat. Maybe a ballad? I've booked the studio for three weeks' time. You should be able to come up with

34

something really good by then, won't you?"

"Yep," said Kasha brightly. "Course." He ended the call, sank down on the steps of the Swan and looked up at the sky.

"What am I going to do?" he asked out loud.

"About what?" asked a familiar voice behind him. "Was the workshop so awful you need celestial help?"

Kasha looked round with a smile on his face. He always had time for Livy Marvell. She came and sat down beside him.

"No, Livy," he said. "The workshop was fine. In fact, Aeysha's song was brilliant. That girl really can write. Not just tunes, lyrics too."

"She's a genius, that's why," said Olivia. "But is everything all right, Kasha? You sounded a bit desperate."

"I was just thinking out loud," said Kasha. "It was nothing really."

"*Nothing will come of nothing*," said Olivia lightly.

Kasha frowned. "Wait, don't tell me..." His face lit up. "*King Lear?*"

Olivia nodded. She read a lot of Shakespeare.

Kasha sighed. "Well, the old boy was right about nothing coming of nothing. My record company just called and they want another song for the album. But they want it, like, yesterday."

"Surely that's not a problem, is it?" replied Olivia. "You've always been so prolific. You used to be able to make up brilliant songs on the spot."

"Not any more," said Kasha bitterly. "The gift has suddenly deserted me." He looked at Olivia. "I am going to tell you something I haven't told anyone else. I haven't written a song for weeks." He put his head in his hands. "I *can't* write one. When I try, all that comes out is rubbish."

"But surely that happens to lots of writers," said Olivia, putting an arm around him. "Isn't it called being blocked? You'll get over that, I know you will."

"Well, I'll have to get over it pretty quick or it's goodbye to my brilliant career," said Kasha, and he looked so worried that Olivia hugged him.

Chapter Six

"Georgia!" called Alex. Georgia whirled round. She bit her lip. She was in a hurry, she knew the others were waiting for her, but she couldn't resist Alex, who was sauntering towards her as if they had all the time in the world and he only had eyes for her.

"Where are you off to in such a hurry?" he asked.

Georgia looked flustered. "Eh, nowhere," she said, unconvincingly.

"I've never noticed Nowhere on the London A-Z," said Alex, with a devastating smile. "Can I come to Nowhere with you? Or aren't I invited?"

Georgia blushed. She had suggested to Olivia and Tom and the others that they invite

Alex along with them to Tower Bridge to see the progress that Jack and Pablo were making, but the others hadn't wanted to. She knew that Aeysha and Katie found him arrogant, Tom hadn't taken to him at all, while Olivia seemed entirely indifferent.

In fact, Olivia was beginning to find Alex Parks a bit annoying. He seemed to have taken her gran's suggestion as an invitation to hang out with them all the time, and he kept looking at her in a way that made her feel as if she had suddenly sprouted a second head. Besides, he wasn't half as good at the high-wire as he seemed to think he was, and although, like a lot of the Swans, she was impressed by his mimicry, she was less impressed by the way he used it. She had recently walked into one of the music practice rooms with Aeysha to find him entertaining Eel, Emmy and some of their friends with a wicked impersonation of Alicia. It had made her feel uncomfortable. So when Georgia had mentioned taking Alex down to Tower Bridge with them, Olivia had frowned and shaken her head.

Seeing Georgia's disappointed face, Tom had said kindly, "Georgie, let's go somewhere without Alex for a change. We don't really know him that well yet, and Jack and Pablo may not like it if we turn up at the river with someone new. Everything's supposed to be under wraps until the announcement."

Aeysha and Katie had murmured in agreement and Georgia hadn't pushed the issue. Now, though, with Alex standing so close to her, looking at her as if she was the only girl in the universe, Georgia wished that she had. Why shouldn't Alex come with them? He was one of the group now. But she knew that if she just turned up with him, the others would be furious.

"Sorry, Alex," she said. "If it was up to me, of course you could come with us. But it's not. Livy's in charge and she's not keen."

"And do you always do what Livy tells you to?" asked Alex, sounding amused.

"Of course not," said Georgia indignantly. "It's just ... it's just that this is her thing."

Alex raised an eyebrow and waited.

"It's something to do with her dad," mumbled Georgia.

"Ah, the great Jack Marvell," said Alex, sounding intrigued. "I was telling my dad about him and how his kids were here at the Swan, and he was really interested."

"Was he?" said Georgia. "Look, I've got to go, the others will be waiting for me."

"You'd better run along then, like a good girl," said Alex. "Unless..." He paused. "Unless you want to hang out with me?"

Georgia's heart gave a leap. Maybe he was interested in her after all? She hardly dared to hope after the way he was always looking at Olivia. How could Livy not notice Alex's smouldering gaze? Every time Alex looked at Georgia, which was not nearly as often as she would have liked, she felt as if his dark eyes were boring into her soul. In her heart, she knew that it was Livy he was interested in. It was so unfair! Livy clearly couldn't care less about him. Maybe if she could just be patient, Alex would get fed up with mooning after Livy, and then she'd be there, waiting for him...

"Well, I suppose I could..." she said hesitantly, but she saw a shadow flit across Alex's face as if he hadn't really expected her to agree to his offer and he was now regretting it.

Georgia felt hurt. "Actually, no," she said, mustering as much dignity as she could. "My friends are waiting for me."

Alex shrugged. "Whatever," he said nonchalantly, but the way he turned his big sorrowful eyes on her reminded Georgia of a hurt puppy and made her feel as if she'd let him down. She was immediately reeled in again like a fish at the end of a line.

"We could meet up later," she said, astonished by her own daring.

"Sorry, Georgie, I'm busy later," said Alex and walked away. She watched him saunter down the corridor and stop to speak to Eel. The two of them seemed to be having a very intense conversation. Georgia wondered what on earth Eel Marvell and Alex Parks had to say to each other.

Georgia walked alongside Olivia and Aeysha as they headed down towards the river. Tom and Katie were a bit ahead. They could see the wire stretched across the river from some distance away.

"I don't know why we couldn't have invited Alex," said Georgia. "He looked really hurt when I said he couldn't come with us."

"You didn't tell him where we were going,

did you?" asked Olivia sharply.

"Of course not," said Georgia crossly. "I know it's a secret." She waved a hand at the wire. "But I don't see why bringing Alex would have hurt. It's obvious *something* is going on down here, it won't be a secret for much longer."

"Probably not," said Olivia, "but Jack wants to try and control the announcement, drum up some press interest. He needs all the publicity he can get. The media are more likely to make a big splash of it that way."

"Since when did you become such a big expert on the media?" said Georgia snappily and she suddenly sped up to join Tom and Katie.

Olivia looked after her, perplexed. "Have I done something to upset Georgie? She's been really crabby with me all term. I don't know what's got into her."

Aeysha hesitated. She was about to say that maybe Olivia needed to be a bit more aware of the situation with Alex, and be a bit more sensitive to her friend's feelings, but Jack and Pablo suddenly appeared and Olivia ran towards them.

"Eel didn't come with you, then?" asked Jack, after he had shown everyone round the site and Olivia had even walked on the wire for a bit. Jack hadn't let her go very far, certainly not beyond the point where it passed out over the shoreline and across the water. He told her that the wind was ferocious in the middle of the wire.

"No," said Olivia. "I did ask her if she wanted to come but she said she was busy. I think she and Emmy must be up to something. She was filling in some kind of form, but she hid it from me when I walked into the room. Probably one of those daft ballet-magazine competitions that she and Emmy are always entering. I hope she hasn't been neglecting you."

"No," smiled Jack. "She was down briefly yesterday. But she caught me at a tricky time so I couldn't give her a lot of attention. We were having a few problems with the rigging so I was rather distracted. She got me to sign some form, a school trip or something, although I don't know why Alicia didn't just do it. Anyway, once I signed it she was away and said she'd try and come back today."

"Maybe she'll bring Emmy with her later," said Olivia.

"Maybe," said Jack. "So, you've pretty well

seen the entire set up. Unless you want to check out the portaloo?" He waved at a small blue structure on the shoreline.

"Phew, it's a relief to see that," said Tom. "I hadn't liked to ask how you were going to, ahem, *go*."

Jack grinned. "It's all accounted for. I have to spend twenty-four hours on the wire for thirty days with up to six ten-minute toilet breaks over any twenty-four hour period. But apart from those breaks, I'm going to cook, eat, perform and sleep entirely on the wire. Well, actually I'll be sleeping in a hammock that I'll rig underneath the wire every night."

"I'm really worried you'll get exhausted. Gran is, too," said Olivia.

"Well, it's an endurance feat as much as anything," said Jack. "I'm not expecting it to be a piece of cake. The thing I'm most worried about is wind. Being buffeted around on the wire day in, day out won't be fun, and it could be quite unpleasant in the hammock at night. I'll just have to make sure I don't fall out."

Olivia shivered as she watched the dark water swirling against the supports of the bridge. "But you will be wearing a safety harness, won't you, Dad, so if you did fall out, you wouldn't plummet into the river and drown?"

Her father laughed. "Of course I will, chick, what do you think I am, mad?"

"I do sometimes," admitted Olivia.

"Ha!" said Tom. "Talk about the pot calling the kettle black!"

Chapter Seven

"Eel! Eel!" Emmy was calling her friend. "Where are you going? You're heading the wrong way for extra tap."

Eel swung round on the stairs. "I'm not coming, Ems."

Emmy's face fell. "But why? You love tap. Are you ill?"

Eel shook her head. "I think I've just gone off it a bit, Emmy. I really want to concentrate on my ballet this term. I've been doing some reading. Lots of people think that if you want to be a ballerina, you need to specialise as soon as possible. Tap, jazz, all those other forms of dance are just a distraction."

Emmy frowned. "But you love them so much."

Eel sighed. "I do, but maybe sometimes you have to make sacrifices to be the best at something."

"My mum says there's plenty of time to specialise. She's going to talk to Miss Swan and Miss Taylor about whether I've got a chance of getting into the Imperial or the Royal Ballet when I'm eleven." Emmy's eyes were shining. "That would be mint. We could go together." She paused. "But I'm not sure I could bear to leave the Swan. I've been here since I was seven. It would be harder still for you, Eel. The Swan's your home. It's lucky we don't have to think about it for a couple of years."

For some reason, Eel seemed to find it difficult to meet her friend's eye. "I've got to go, Ems, I'll see you tomorrow." She turned and continued walking up the stairs towards the flat. Emmy stared after her, a hurt and slightly puzzled look on her face. Why was Eel behaving so strangely?

Once in the flat, Eel checked that nobody else was around, went into her bedroom and closed the door behind her. She felt bad about Emmy. Having a secret she couldn't share meant that she had to keep pushing her best friend away. She hated that.

She felt under the mattress of her bed and pulled out the large, thick cream envelope. Just holding it felt exciting. She had poured over the prospectus for the Imperial with its pictures of eager-faced children at the barre and the elegant swan-necked older pupils. There was something thrilling about thinking that one day she might be amongst their number.

Eel pulled out the prospectus and carefully took out the application form. It was signed and dated by Jack on the final page. Seeing his signature made her feel shabby because she had lied to him to get it. For a moment, she hesitated. Then she took a deep breath and began to finish filling in the form in her best handwriting. She knew what she was doing was sneaky and wrong, but she just had to know whether she really did have the talent to be a ballerina. If Gran and Miss Taylor wouldn't tell her, then auditioning for the Imperial was the only way she was going to find out.

Chapter Eight

"How happy some o'er other some can be!
Through Athens I am thought as fair as she.
But what of that? Demetrius thinks not so;
He will not know what all but he do know..."

Georgia continued to the end of the speech from Act One of *A Midsummer Night's Dream*. Georgia, as Helena, was expressing her despair that the boy she really liked, Demetrius, only had eyes for her friend, Hermia. Everyone was spellbound, including Olivia, who had been cast as Hermia. She glanced at Connor, who was playing Lysander. He seemed to be completely mesmerised by Georgia's performance.

Only Alex, who was playing Demetrius, appeared not to be gripped. He was riffling through his script, looking bored. There was a tiny silence as Georgia reached the end of the speech before the final bell for the afternoon rang. The class broke into delighted applause.

"Thank you, Georgia," said Sebastian Shaw, "that was lovely. It really felt as if you were feeling every single word. And thank you, Livy, Con and Alex, too. The scene is really coming together. Well done all of you. We'll move on to the Fairy scenes tomorrow, so anyone involved in those needs to check over their lines tonight and make sure they are word perfect. You can't put the effort into acting if you are putting it into remembering the script."

Olivia went to get her bag, which was hanging over the back of her chair. She saw Alex looking at her intently, but she ignored him and grinned at Tom, who winked back at her. Alex was *really* getting on her nerves. Even little things he did irritated her, but worst of all was the fact that he called her Liv. Jack and Tom were the only people in the world who were allowed to call her that. Even Eel had always called her Livy.

Olivia and the others crowded into the corridor, which was full of Swans heading towards the cloakrooms, either to gather their things and head for home or to change for the extra dance, music or circus workshops that they took after school. Georgia had been waylaid by Connor who was talking to her quietly but passionately. She was shaking her head, and kept giving sideways glances towards Alex as if she was eager to get away.

Aeysha and Katie peeled off for the girls' cloakrooms.

"Georgia was great as Helena, wasn't she?" said Katie generously.

'Yes," said Aeysha. "Funny and sad at the same time, and so completely lovelorn." She hesitated, then said, "But I'm not sure it was all acting."

"I did wonder," said Katie.

"If you think about it," said Aeysha, "the beginning of *A Midsummer Night's Dream* is a bit like real life at the moment. Georgia's keen on Alex who only has eyes for Olivia. In *Dream*, Helena wants Demetrius who wants Hermia who isn't interested in him. Mr Shaw's casting is spot on."

"Are you quite sure Livy isn't interested in Alex?" asked Katie. "She's not just playing it really cool?"

Aeysha shook her head. "I don't think she knows how to play it cool, it's not Livy's style at all. She always wears her heart on her sleeve, and anyway, I'm sure she would have told one of us if she was interested in Alex. She's just too busy doing her own stuff on the wire and trapeze and worrying about Jack to give him a second thought. But the thing is, I suspect her total lack of interest is probably a big part of her appeal. I guess Alex Parks isn't used to being ignored by girls."

"I can see why," said Katie, "although he's not my type. Too full of himself."

"Alex is used to having girls swooning all over him," continued Aeysha, "but then along comes Livy who's lovely and not in the slightest bit interested. She's a challenge!"

"Whereas Georgia is completely gorgeous, but no challenge at all."

"Precisely," said Aeysha. "But you know what really worries me?" Katie shook her head. "In *A Midsummer Night's Dream*, Helena and Hermia's friendship is almost destroyed. I couldn't bear it if that happened to Livy and Georgia. It would ruin everything. No boy, and particularly not Mr full-of-himself Alex Parks, is worth falling out with one of your best friends."

The two girls went out of the cloakroom.

"There you are!" said Olivia. "Are you two going to your contemporary class?"

"Yes," said Aeysha.

"Do you want to meet up at the café after?"

They nodded.

"Great," said Olivia. "Because I'm going to help Pablo with after-school high-wire."

"I'm just on my way there now," smiled Alex, who had suddenly appeared behind them. "I'll walk with you, Liv."

Olivia started to shrug, but remembered her manners. "OK." But then she suddenly turned back. "Oh, sorry Alex, I've just remembered I need a quick word with Tom. Don't wait for me, I'll catch you up."

"Do you want me to take your bag for you, Liv?" asked Alex, eagerly.

A look of puzzlement crossed Olivia's face. "Why on earth would you want to do that?" she asked.

Aeysha and Katie watched Olivia and Alex walk in different directions, then burst out laughing.

"Oh dear," said Aeysha. "If it wasn't for poor Georgia's feelings, it would be really funny. Better than a play, almost."

Chapter Nine

"Eel! Eel!" There was no answer. Olivia had looked in all Eel's usual haunts and hadn't found her, and eventually she had gone up to the flat on the off-chance that Eel had slipped up there at lunch time for some reason. She had passed her Gran on the stairs and had asked her if she knew where Eel was.

"Probably with Emmy," replied Alicia. But Olivia had found Emmy in the dance studio with some of her other friends and had asked her if she knew where her little sister was. Emmy had shaken her head. "She keeps going off on her own," she'd said a little sadly. "She's even given up coming to extra tap. I thought she must be really sick to miss extra tap. But she said that she was just giving tap a bit of a rest for a while."

Olivia had looked at Emmy's wan face. "You two haven't fallen out, have you?" she'd asked gently.

Emmy had shaken her head hard. "No, that's why I don't understand it. It's as if she's thinking about something else all the time and just wants to be alone."

Olivia had frowned. Wanting to be alone was not typical Eel behavior at all. She was never happier than when she was in a crowd. Olivia loved being with Tom, Georgia and the others but she could quite happily spend hours on her own practising the high wire or reading Shakespeare or even just day-dreaming. Jack always said that if his daughters had been animals Eel would definitely have been a dog and Olivia a cat. "Probably a wild cat," he added with a grin. "A puma or a snow leopard."

"Listen, Emmy," Olivia had said, smiling reassuringly. "I expect it's just a phase she's going through. You've always been her best friend."

Olivia walked back out of the flat, closed the door carefully behind her to ensure it was locked and went downstairs again. She thought she would just check in the music rooms and after that she would head to the river without Eel, even though she had promised Jack that she would bring her little sister with her.

She stopped outside one of the music rooms. The door was closed but she could hear voices from within. To her astonishment, she realised that the voices belonged to Eel and Alicia.

Alicia was saying: "I know it's unusual but I hope you understand the situation. I would be very grateful," and then Eel replied excitedly: "That's perfect! Completely perfect."

Olivia frowned. Why hadn't her gran said she was on her way to talk to Eel? She supposed that Alicia must have just found Eel in the music room. But there was something about the exchange that struck her as odd, though she couldn't quite put her finger on it. Olivia pushed open the door. Two faces swung guiltily around, and Oliva found herself staring at Eel and Alex. They both looked put out to be discovered together.

"What are you up to?" she asked, a sharp edge to her voice.

"Nothing," said Eel quickly.

Olivia glared at Alex. "I heard you

impersonating my gran again."

Alex fixed his soulful eyes on Olivia. "I didn't mean anything by it, I really respect Miss Swan. She's an amazing woman. I was just entertaining your little sister, Liv."

"Well, she doesn't need entertaining. She's supposed to be coming with me to see Dad."

"Maybe I can tag along," said Alex, and it sounded like a statement not a question.

"Oh Alex, of course you can," said Eel enthusiastically. "I'm sure Dad would like to meet you."

"Sorry," said Olivia brusquely. "This is a Marvell-only outing. Maybe another time."

"I'll look forward to it," said Alex. "It would be nice to spend some time with you, Liv."

"Actually," said Olivia, with a forced smile, "I'd really like it if you didn't call me Liv. Livy or Olivia is just fine."

For a second a brief look of astonishment mixed with hurt flitted across Alex's face, and then he recovered himself. "I'll remember that, Livy. Sorry."

He winked at Eel. "See you around, Eel. It's nice doing business with you."

* * *

Olivia hurried towards the river with Eel trying to keep up.

"What did he mean, 'nice doing business with you'?" asked Olivia.

Eel reddened. "It's nothing. Just a turn of phrase," she said.

"You're not up to something, are you? You're neglecting Emmy. She seems quite hurt."

Eel bristled. "You're one to talk about upsetting your friends!" she said.

"What on earth do you mean?" asked Olivia.

Eel sighed. "Sometimes I think you're completely blind, Livy. You never notice anything. It's *so* obvious to everyone else. It's the talk of the school!"

"What's so obvious?" asked Olivia impatiently, speeding up until Eel was all but running.

"I can't believe I have to tell you," said Eel. "Georgia is soft on Alex."

"Oh," said Olivia. "Well, I had noticed she behaves very oddly when he's around, and she does want to drag him along to everything. Maybe she should ask him out?" Olivia frowned. "Although, it would be very odd if one of us started going out with someone. Actually, I don't think I'd like that very much at all. I like it as we are. Me, Tom, Aeysha, Georgia and Katie. Although things are going to change next year when Aeysha leaves. It won't feel the same at all."

"Well, Alex and Georgia are never going to happen," said Eel, "because Alex is interested in someone else."

"Who?" asked Olivia.

Eel gave a long sigh of disbelief. "You, of course, dummy."

Olivia stopped walking. "Me? Don't be silly, Eel. Alex Parks and I have got absolutely nothing in common. In fact, I think he's a bit creepy. It's as if he's *acting* being really nice all the time rather than *really* being nice. Sometimes when he looks at me I feel as if I'm being engulfed by an oil slick."

Eel giggled. "I think he's trying to be charming, and it's clear there are plenty of other Swan girls who find that kind of thing attractive." She paused. "Livy, maybe you should tell him? Not that you think that he's an oil slick, obviously, but that you're not interested. I think he thinks he's in with a chance." She paused and looked embarrassed. "In fact, he asked me if I'd put in a good word with you for him, and I promised I would."

Olivia looked horrified. "So that's what the two of you were doing together," she said, angrily.

"Er, sort of, yes," said Eel, looking shifty. "But Livy, it's clearly a hopeless cause. You should tell him he's wasting his time."

"I think I'd better. I feel terrible about Georgia. It's explains why she's so snappy with me. Maybe if I tell Alex I'm not interested, it will clear the way for her."

"Maybe," said Eel doubtfully.

"Eel," said Olivia. "I feel like such a total noodle for not noticing. Thanks for telling me."

"Oh, that's OK," said Eel. "You're welcome to ask your little sister's advice any time you like. Though I may have to start charging. Maybe I could set myself up as an agony aunt."

At that moment they passed the tube station where the free evening paper was just being delivered. Olivia took one off the top of the pile and unfolded it to look at the headline. She gasped.

High-Wire Daredevil Preparing River Thames

Stunt!

Fury rose in her throat. Somehow word about Jack's plans had got out! She quickly scanned the story, and then immediately she realised that she was wrong. It was even worse than she thought. The newspaper wasn't referring to Jack at all. The story was about the Russian stunt man, Viktor Ivanov, who planned to perform the exact same stunt as Jack a mile or so down the river from him at exactly the same time! Olivia felt sick. Jack had been wrong when he said he'd been given permission instead of his rival. They had both been given it! Jack had competition, and the first round had gone to the Russian.

Eel saw her sister's white face. "What is it, Livy?" she asked. Olivia passed her the newspaper soundlessly.

The two girls studied the picture of Viktor Ivanov, who looked very young but very determined. The article also broke the news of Jack's attempt, and included a quote from Viktor's agent, Ethan Rees. Olivia read it aloud, her voice becoming angrier and angrier: " 'The Great Marvello is yesterday's news. Viktor is a rising star. This will be a battle between two gladiators played out on the high-wire suspended above the Thames. And my boy will be victorious.' "

Olivia was so outraged that she made Eel run all the rest of the way to the river. But when they arrived, Pablo was already on the phone with Ethan Rees.

"Listen, don't worry, Liv," said Jack. "It's a game. They're just trying to psych me out with all that talk of me being past it. As far as I'm concerned, the more the merrier. The rivalry between us will stir up more interest in the stunt. It's just a pity that this Viktor guy has got in first, but I certainly don't want to get in a fight with the guy. There's room for both of us on the river. It's just a bit of showmanship, that's all."

When Pablo came off the phone, he agreed with Jack. "The rivalry will be good for both your dad and this young upstart. Especially when Jack wins! I just wish I'd thought of it myself." He turned to Jack. "Ethan Rees wants to hold a joint press conference next week. It will be a bit like the weigh-in before a boxing bout. He wants us to play up the competitiveness, go for a bit of banter. What do you think?"

Jack looked pensive, and Olivia felt a surge

of sympathy for him. She knew that kind of flashy posturing wasn't Jack's thing.

"You don't have to do it, Dad," she said, gently.

"I think it sounds fun," said Eel. "Like a mock duel. Exciting."

"Eel's probably right," said Jack. "It's just a bit of fun." He looked at Olivia's serious face. "Don't you worry about me, chick. I'll be fine. Viktor the whippersnapper had better look out. I feel quite sorry for him already."

Pablo grinned. "I'll tell Ethan we're up for it."

But Olivia was worried. She didn't want Jack to take any more risks than were necessary and she knew that if Viktor and his manager started upping the stakes, Jack would match them all the way.

"Don't be anxious, little duckling," whispered Pablo. "This Viktor Ivanov is an amateur compared with the Great Marvello!"

Chapter Ten

The buzz in the auditorium at Campion's Palace of Varieties was growing louder and more excited. The space was full of journalists and camera crews. One of the sponsors had laid on free fizzy wine and sandwiches, which were disappearing fast. It was lunchtime and, with Alicia's permission, Olivia, Eel and their friends had left school so they could be at Jack's press conference. Two large screens on either side of the stage were showing some of both men's previous exploits. There was film of Jack crossing Niagara Falls and Snake Canyon, and the other screen showed Viktor doing a complicated stunt on the top of a moving train in a low -budget Russian movie and jumping a tank of sharks on a motor bike.

"Hmm," said Eel. "The sharks are the ones looking scared silly."

"So," said Aeysha, watching the films, "has this guy actually done any high-wire walking?"

Olivia and Tom nodded. "He's a jack of all trades. He's scaled some of Moscow's highest buildings without climbing aids, and he's done some dangerous stunts with fireworks. He's even been a human canon ball, and yes, he's done some high-wire stuff, too," said Tom. "We looked at some of it on YouTube."

"His tricking is pretty good, but not as good as Jack's," said Olivia. "The main thing is that it's all high performance, short duration stuff. What he and Jack are trying to do now isn't just about stunts, it's about real endurance. And Dad's got plenty of experience of that."

A triumphant march started to play over the loud speakers. The screen at the back of the stage was flashing "Clash of the Titans" and the words "Day Zero". The compère was more used to introducing boxers and darts players, and he spoke in the odd whoopy way that was typical of such MCs.

The music changed, and the compère shouted loudly: "Put your hands together for the man on my right, the Great Marvello, action hero and man of courage, the amazing, the peerless, the unsurpassed, the supreme stunt man and high-wire walker ... Jack Marvell!" He made the last syllable of Marvell sound like a long drawn-out war cry.

Jack walked on to the stage. His hands were raised above his head but his broad smile seemed a little bashful as he acknowledged the applause and the cheers of the audience. He was wearing the slightly battered dark-blue cloak covered in tiny silver stars that he had worn as Prospero in the Swan Circus show *Enchantment* at the Edinburgh Festival the previous summer. Mixed in amongst the cheers were a few boos. Olivia's head whipped round to see where they were coming from, but Tom put a restraining hand on her arm.

"Don't worry about it, Liv. It doesn't mean anything. It's just part of the show."

"Well," said Olivia indignantly, "it all seems a bit of a circus to me." She burst out laughing when she realised what she'd said, and Tom and the others joined in.

New music started playing, booming and jubilant. The compère began to speak again.

"And on my left, the unparalleled stuntman phenomenon that is the extraordinary, the lion-hearted, the incredible, the death-defying, shark-jumping prodigy and challenger all the way from the icy Russian Steppes, Viktor the Viktorious!" As the final words died away the music built to a crescendo and Viktor walked on stage with a swagger. He was an extraordinary sight. He was dressed in a silver jumpsuit with a thick belt around his waist studded with gems. His shoulders were padded like an American footballer, his cloak was made of lush, red velvet and as he turned round, the words "Viktor the Viktorious" could be spotted picked out in diamante on the back.

Olivia thought he looked completely daft, but saw that his eyes were wary despite the big smile on his face. The crowd went crazy and the camera men pushed each other out of the way to get a better position for their shots. Viktor played to the crowd much more than Jack and it took a full couple of minutes before everyone settled.

The compère turned to Jack.

"Are you ready for the Clash of the Titans?"

"Raring to go," said Jack. The Swans cheered.

"What do you say to those who think you're over the hill and won't last the distance?"

"I say they are very wrong," said Jack. "I'm not even in my prime! It's going to be tough. But I'll still be there at the end."

Some people at the back started to chant. "Has-been. Has-been. Has-been."

"How rude!" said Aeysha. Olivia saw Pablo's face. He looked horrified.

The compère turned to Viktor. "What about you – the newcomer. Do you have the experience to make it to the end of this mighty feat of endurance?"

Viktor did a little shuffle and a twirl. "What do you think?" he said, his words tinged with a slight accent. "Look at me, I can take anything that old man throws at me. I'm going to win!"

"Don't be so sure of that," said Jack, with a grin.

"Bring it on, daddy," said Viktor. "Don't worry about me, old man." He skipped about like a spring lamb and pretended to box Jack.

"Oh well, as they say, getting old is

obligatory but growing up is optional," retorted Jack.

Viktor drew himself up to his full height, and raised his arms. "Viktor will be victorious!" The people at the back cheered wildly and Jack looked increasingly uncomfortable as the chant of "Viktor! Viktor!" grew louder and louder.

After it was all over, the Swans sat in one of the dressing rooms with Jack and Pablo. They all looked gloomy.

"I'm sorry, Jack," said Pablo. "I under-estimated Ethan Rees' bloodlust." Then he added, darkly, "And the depth of his pockets. He obviously paid those people to boo you and cheer Viktor."

"It doesn't matter," said Jack, stoically. "What matters is what happens out on the wire."

Olivia knew that her dad was right, but she couldn't help thinking that not only had Rees and Viktor won the first round, they had scored a convincing win in the second bout, too.

In the little dressing room on the other side of the stage, Viktor was miserably biting his fingernails.

"I can't bear it, Ethan. Jack Marvell has always been a real hero to me. He's no has-been."

"Listen, my boy," said Ethan, "in this business you've got to grab any advantage that you can. There is no such thing as rules, only winning. And you are going to win, Viktor. And when you do, the world will be your oyster. Hollywood movies, the works. You want that, don't you?"

Viktor nodded.

"That's my boy," said Ethan. "I've invested a lot in you, Viktor, and you're going to triumph. I'm going to make sure that you do. And if that means bringing Jack Marvell down, so be it. I've nothing against the man but there can only be one winner and my job is to make sure that winner is you."

Ethan's phone began to chirp. He looked at it. "Ah," he said. "One of the favours I'm calling in on your behalf." He put the phone to his ear and headed out of the door.

Viktor watched him disappear and sighed loudly. Of course he wanted to win. But he wanted to do it fair and square. He wanted to do it the way that he knew Jack Marvell would do it, with grace and honour. He was beginning to realise that wasn't how Ethan Rees saw things. But he couldn't back out now.

Chapter Eleven

There was a carnival atmosphere down by the river, where even a band was playing. Although it was still early, several thousand people had gathered to watch Jack take his first steps on to the wire that would be his home for the next thirty days. Tower Bridge was crammed with people. Even the London mayor had stopped by, and he had delighted the onlookers when, with Pablo's help and wearing a fetching harness, he had tottered a couple of steps on to the wire that extended over the Thames at a height slightly higher than a double-decker bus. In truth, the crowd was all rather hoping that the accident-prone mayor would fall in, but he retreated safely off the wire and made a little speech saying that he hoped the best man would win.

Olivia glanced around. All her friends were here with her and Eel and Alicia. But she could see some other Swans in the crowd too. She could see Emmy and her whole family, as well as Connor and Kylie who were heading their way.

Further back she was a little surprised to spot Alex Parks, standing talking to a man about Jack's age and build, who she guessed must be his dad. A woman in a wheelchair was with them and Olivia remembered that Alex had said his mum was sick. The man was talking very intently to Alex, who kept shaking his head as if he was disagreeing strongly with his dad about something.

After a few minutes, Alex stormed away from his dad and started working his way through the crowd towards Olivia's group. Georgia saw him coming and gave him a welcoming smile, but just at that moment Connor slipped into the space beside her, so Alex had to hover on the edge of the group.

A news helicopter was hovering overhead and several boats laden with journalists and photographers were circling directly under the wire stretching across the river. Hanging from it were several large pouches containing the things that Jack would need over the coming days: food and cooking equipment, extra wet-weather gear and some of the equipment he wanted for stunts. He would restock during his toilet breaks.

A blonde TV reporter was doing a piece to camera. "There is great excitement here by Tower Bridge as Jack Marvell, also known as the Great Marvello, prepares to step out on to the high-wire. He will be spending thirty days and nights suspended over the Thames in a feat of endurance described by some experts as impossible. Interest in the stunt has been made all the greater because, just a mile down the river, the Russian stuntman who goes by the name Viktor Viktorious is attempting an identical feat. A joint press conference held yesterday suggested that the rivalry between the two men is intense. Which will endure – youth or experience?"

The reporter signed off and handed over to her colleague who was on the river at Waterloo, waiting for the moment when Viktor would also step out on to the wire for the very first time.

Jack turned to Olivia, Eel and Alicia.

"Right then," he said. "Time to say goodbye for the next month or so."

Alicia stepped forward and gave him a hug and a peck on the cheek. "Good luck, Jack. You know my views on this mad stunt. But I know you can't be stopped so just make sure you take good care of yourself out on that wire." She stepped back to allow Olivia and Eel a chance to have a quiet moment with their dad.

Jack hugged both the girls. "Now you be good for your grandmother," he said.

"I'm going to come down every day to see you," said Olivia fiercely.

"That would be lovely, chick," said Jack. "But I won't hold you to it. I'm going to be out there for a month and you'll both be busy with your lives."

Eel gulped. "You will take care, Dad, won't you?"

"No risks," said Jack. "I promise."

"Not even if this Viktor takes them," said Olivia anxiously. "It doesn't matter if he gets more attention than you. Even if he does succeed in staying on the wire for the full time and you don't, we won't love you any the less."

"I know that, Liv, of course. I always know

that whatever I do. But I'm not worried about Viktor. I'm not sure he's got the stamina to last thirty days."

"Me neither," said Pablo. "Come on, Jack, time to get this show on the road."

Jack gave Olivia and Eel one last hug and walked towards the wire. When he got to the end he clipped on a safety harness. He then produced a unicycle and a bowler hat and, instead of just stepping out on to the wire as everyone expected, he cycled across the river. The crowd cheered.

There was an electronic screen at the side of the river that read "Day One", and underneath it ticked away to show how many days and hours and seconds were yet to go. When Jack reached the middle of the wire he bent down to one of the pouches, produced a copy of the *Guardian* and sat nonchalantly on the unicycle reading it as if it was the most relaxing thing in the world to hang out on a wire reading the paper. The crowd cheered again.

"Pablo," said Olivia, "what makes you think that Viktor won't be able to go the distance?"

"Well," said Pablo, "I reckon he might

have underestimated quite how exhausting being out there on the river night and day will be, particularly as..." Pablo stopped as if he felt he was saying too much.

"Particularly as what?" asked Olivia.

"Look, Livy, I don't want to worry you, but the long-range weather forecast is dreadful. High winds and bitterly cold conditions. Maybe even hail and snow." Olivia stared at him, her eyes anxious. Pablo tried to smile reassuringly. "Don't worry, Livy, your dad is as tough as old boots."

Chapter Twelve

Eel looked nervously around the great pearly-hued marble hall with its sweeping staircase that was like something out of a 1930s Fred Astaire and Ginger Rogers movie. The windows on the staircase had small panes of coloured blue glass separated by dark leading. Everything at the Imperial was on a grand scale and the imposing surroundings made Eel feel very small, like Alice after she drank the shrinking potion. She began to think this might not have been such a good idea after all.

It was a Saturday morning and she had told Alicia that she had been invited to spend the day with Emmy and her family. There had been a tricky moment when Alicia had said that she would walk her round, but Eel told her that Olivia had already offered. She hated lying to her gran. It made her feel like a criminal. She thought she had been so clever: arranging her own audition, filling in all the forms and creeping around getting to the post before her dad or Gran saw it. Not that it had been difficult with Jack. He had been out in the morning long before the post came and only got back after dark, so she had had plenty of time to snaffle anything addressed to him from the Imperial. Fortunately, the Imperial letters came in distinctive thick cream envelopes with "Imperial Ballet School" clearly marked on them so she knew what to look for. But now she was here she wished she had a grown-up to support her. Maybe it had all been a big mistake. Maybe she should just go home.

She looked up at the great domed ceiling and the dark wooden boards on which the names of the graduating pupils who had won the annual Imperial prize were etched in fine gold lettering. Eel wondered whether her name might be there one day and a little girl coming for an audition would recognise it and say to her parents, "Look! The greatest ballerina of them all studied at the Imperial!"

Eel gave a little shiver of excitement and fear. She felt that she was taking a step into the unknown. In the distance, she could hear some music that made her feet want to dance. The sensation settled her stomach and she stopped hopping nervously from foot to foot in front of the registrar's dark wooden desk, which had clearly been set up in the hallway for the audition day.

The registrar peered over her glasses at Eel and frowned. "Alicia Ophelia Rosalind Marvell? You're definitely on the list but it's all most irregular. I don't think we've ever had a child turn up for an audition without at least one adult with them. Have you really nobody with you?"

Eel shook her chestnut curls so she looked like an eager spaniel. "My mum's dead, and my dad is spending thirty days and nights on a high-wire above the Thames, so he couldn't come." Eel leaned forward confidentially. "You can't get time off work if doing that kind of thing is your job."

The registrar looked interested and considered Eel more closely. "I've read about that in the papers. It sounds mad. So are you

Jack Marvell's daughter?"

Eel nodded again. "I've always thought he was rather dashing," said the registrar.

Eel wrinkled her nose. "I suppose he might be to some people, but to me he's just my dad. I know he would be here if he could, and he did sign the form." She pointed at the paper that the registrar had in front of her. "And," added Eel, "my grandmother, Alicia Swan, spoke to Miss Popova and explained I'd have to come on my own because she's busy today and I don't really have any other relatives except for my uncle and cousin and they live in Edinburgh, which is miles away."

"Oh," said the registrar. "So Alicia Swan is your grandmother? I'll just give Miss Popova a call, maybe she can shed some light on the situation." She picked up her phone. "Why don't you sit over there for a moment, Alicia."

"Actually, nobody calls me Alicia, everyone calls me Eel," said Eel, and then she added helpfully, "because I wriggle a lot."

The registrar raised her eyebrows and murmured, "Even more irregular," but her amused smile was kind.

Eel sat on a chair swinging her feet, clasping her vanity case and watching as more and more girls arrived, their voices echoing around the great hall. The boys' auditions had been held on a different day. Eel felt worried. She had never imagined that there would be so many other children at the audition.

After a few minutes, a graceful woman with her hair scraped back from her face in a bun glided down the stairs. She said something to the registrar who nodded at Eel. The woman walked over to Eel, who stood up. She wondered if she ought to curtsey, but instead found her hand being grasped warmly.

"I am Anna Popova," said the woman, with the faintest trace of a Russian accent. "So you are Eel Marvell. Your grandmother mentioned you to me a few months ago when we were together at a reception for the Russian Ballet. She has great faith in your gift."

"Does she?" said Eel. If Alicia rated her enough to talk to the great Anna Popova about her, she must think she had real talent. Maybe she did have what it takes to be a prima ballerina?

"Today we will test that gift," said Anna Popova. "I will take you through to the changing room with the others where you can get ready. Your grandmother rang me to say that you would be unaccompanied, and although it is not usually the way we do things at the Imperial I am happy to make an exception in your case. I know from past experience that Swan pupils are always mature and professional."

"I'll do my best," said Eel, in a small voice.

"Good, I'd expect nothing less from a Swan," said Anna Popova. "By the way, I hope your grandmother is better."

"Better?" said Eel, confused. She didn't know that Alicia had been ill.

"The terrible laryngitis. When she called me, I said that she didn't sound quite like herself, and she said her throat had been bad for a week and that's why she couldn't talk long."

"Oh, yes," said Eel quickly. "Her throat. It's much better, thank you."

She followed Anna Popova into the changing rooms, which smelled comfortingly familiar to Eel; the odour of antiseptic and sweaty feet also characterised the Swan changing rooms, and Eel thought it was probably a feature of dance-school changing rooms the world over.

She had come out in a cold sweat when Anna Popova had mentioned laryngitis. The trouble with deception was that you had to keep on top of all the lies. It was exhausting, and made Eel feel a bit grubby, as if she hadn't washed properly that morning.

Chapter Thirteen

On Saturday morning, a rehearsal for *A Midsummer Night's Dream* was underway on the Campion's stage. Ella Campion, who owned the beautiful old Victorian music hall, and her friend, Arthur Tuttons, were delighted to have the Swans back again, even though this production was not on nearly such a lavish scale as *Cinderella* had been.

"It is beautiful, though," said Ella, watching Olivia and Georgia sit side by side on the two garlanded swings in the middle of the stage. Behind them, fairies peeped out from a bower of roses entwined with tiny glittering fairy lights. The girls were wearing 1930s-style costumes. Olivia had a calf-length dove-grey skirt and jacket, offset by a vivid green blouse and she was wearing button boots and a jaunty little hat with a feather on its side. Georgia was wearing a floaty floral dress and two strings of pearls. As the play continued, both girls would become more and more dishevelled as the night in the forest transformed them physically and emotionally.

"It's not so much an Athenian forest as an English garden," said Ella.

Sebastian nodded. "That's the idea."

"I love the swings," said Ella.

"Not entirely original, I'm afraid," said Sebastian ruefully. "I rather stole the idea from a famous 1960s production by Peter Brook."

"Oh, I've seen pictures of the one you mean," said Ella. "But that's quite austere. This looks so much prettier. You haven't stolen, you've been inspired to make something new out of it."

"That's what I keep telling myself," said Sebastian. He clapped his hands together. "Everybody to their places, please."

The rehearsal began, occasionally stopping for Sebastian to give a note or make a slight change to the blocking.

Olivia watched from the wings as Alex, as

Demetrius, walked on to the stage followed by Georgia, as Helena, stumbling after him.

Demetrius began to speak:

"I love thee not, therefore pursue me not.
Where is Lysander and fair Hermia?
The one I'll slay, the other slayeth me.
Thou told'st me they were stolen unto this wood;
And here am I, and wood within this wood,
Because I cannot meet my Hermia.
Hence, get thee gone, and follow me no more."

Georgia's eyes flashed with passion:

"You draw me, you hard-hearted adamant;
But yet you draw not iron, for my heart
Is true as steel: leave you your power to draw,
And I shall have no power to follow you."

Demetrius retorted:

"Do I entice you? Do I speak you fair?
Or, rather, do I not in plainest truth
Tell you, I do not, nor I cannot love you?"

Georgia's eyes filled with tears as she launched into her next speech. Olivia thought she had never seen Georgia act so well; the tension between her and Alex was electric.

Olivia had been putting off the dreaded moment when she had to tell Alex that she had no interest in him and he should stop pursuing her. The idea of talking to him about it made her stomach churn. What if Eel was wrong? What if she had got completely the wrong end of the stick and Alex wasn't interested in her at all? She'd feel like a complete idiot. She could imagine him sneering as he said patronisingly that, sorry, but she just wasn't the kind of girl he'd be interested in. She was certain he was the kind of boy to make sure the whole school heard what had taken place. But she couldn't go any longer seeing Georgia unhappy, even if it was doing wonders for her acting. The scene came to an end.

"Fabulous," said Sebastian Shaw. "It's been a good morning's work. Thank you very much for your time, everyone, and please say thanks to Ella and Arthur for putting up with us."

Everyone said thank you and went to pick up their bags. Olivia knew that Georgia was being collected by her dad and going to spend the rest of the weekend with him, his new wife, Leonie, and their new baby, Rosie. She hung back a little until Georgia had left, keeping an eye on Alex who appeared to be in no hurry either. She picked up her things and wandered out into Hangman's Alley, where most of the buildings were still derelict and boarded up. She heard Alex following her and walked slowly down the alleyway to give him time to fall into step beside her.

"Hey, Olivia," said Alex, casually. "Fancy coming down to the river to take a look at what your dad is up to?"

Olivia shook her head. "I'm going down later when he's due one of his bathroom breaks so we'll get a few minutes together."

"I could come down then," said Alex, hopefully.

Suddenly Olivia felt sorry for him. "Alex," she said very seriously. "I think we've got to get something sorted out between us. I'm ... I'm..."

"I've always thought you were really gorgeous, Livy Marvell, from the first moment I saw you," said Alex softly.

Olivia cringed inside. This wasn't going the way she had hoped. "Look Alex, I'm really flattered, of course I am, but I'm just not interested. I don't know how to put it more kindly, but you and me, nothing is ever going to happen between us."

"It's the high-wire, isn't it?" said Alex. "I'm just not good enough at it for you."

"Don't be silly," said Olivia. "Of course it's not that. In fact, you're getting better. You should keep it up. "

"I will," said Alex. "I'll never give up. Not on the wire or on you."

"Oh, Alex," said Olivia, exasperated. "Haven't you heard a word I've been saying?"

"I have, but I don't believe you," said Alex, with his lazy smile. "You're just playing hard to get."

Olivia's eyes widened in irritation . "You're so arrogant, Alex Parks! I wouldn't go out with you if you were the last boy left at the Swan." She stalked off, fuming.

Alex stared after her. No girl had ever spoken to him like that before. Even when he'd been in primary school, he'd always been confident that girls liked him. He felt angry and humiliated. He looked around quickly to check that nobody had witnessed what had happened and was relieved to see that nobody from the Swan was near. It would have been so embarrassing. Anyway, who was Olivia Marvell to think she was so special? It wasn't even as if she was obviously pretty like Georgia, Katie and lots of the other girls at the Swan. She should be grateful that he'd taken notice of her. He wanted to hurt her for making him feel small.

"You'll regret it, Olivia Marvell. Just you wait and see," called Alex, staring hard after her. Olivia didn't reply, she didn't even turn round but just kept walking fast. She couldn't see his face so she couldn't work out whether his words were a plea or a threat. Either way, they made her feel shaky. She hurried her step, eager to put some distance between herself and Alex in case he decided to come after her.

"Well, Olivia Marvell," she said to herself, "you handled that really well, I don't think."

Alex watched her go, his anger rising. He felt in his pocket for his phone and pressed a button.

"Dad," he said. "You know that thing you asked me to help you with if I could?" He paused. "Well, I'm up for it after all."

Chapter Fourteen

Eel watched a girl called Esme complete her solo. She was very good, quite brilliant in fact. Not just technically proficient, but passionate too, as if she didn't just hear the music but felt every note. Everyone at the audition was so good that Eel was finding it a little daunting. There were some fantastic dancers at the Swan in many different disciplines, but there were few who felt as passionately about ballet as Eel. Most were all-rounders with their sights set on a future in musical theatre or possibly contemporary dance as they got older. So Eel was an exception at the Swan, but here she was just one among many children who all felt about ballet as passionately as she did.

She sighed. She probably didn't stand a chance of getting in. She wondered if she had made a big mistake in applying. She was beginning to think that Alicia and India Taylor had had a point when they'd said it was too early to know the extent of her talent. If she had waited until it was time to think about what she would do after Year Six at the Swan, she'd have had so many more lessons. She thought back to the thick creamy brochure that she had pored over in secret in her bedroom. She remembered where it said that "we are not looking for polished dancers but for those who can demonstrate their passion and potential for ballet." Eel looked around the room at all the other would-be prima ballerinas. She would just have to prove her passion and potential was as great as theirs, or even greater.

"Alicia Marvell?" came a voice.

Esme prodded her in the ribs, and Eel jumped.

"That's you," hissed Esme.

Eel smiled gratefully at her and stepped forward to perform the brief solo that she had prepared. She was the last child on the list. Earlier that morning, the girls had all done a class together and been told that after lunch some children would be invited to take part in a further class and some would be going home. Eel guessed this was her last chance to impress or she would be among those out at lunchtime.

The music began and Eel began to dance. As soon as she did, she forgot everything else. She had the sensation of weightlessness that she often experienced when she danced. It was like the dreams she had sometimes of flying over the city of London, looking down at the great dark river and all the famous landmarks. Then, before she knew it, the dance was over, somebody said, "Thank you, Alicia," and she was taking her place next to Esme again.

Anna Popova and the Imperial's dance teachers, who had been watching the children perform, were whispering together. Eel knew it was crunch time. It felt as if her insides had decided to do a tap dance.

After what seemed like a lifetime, Anna Popova and the other teachers stood up. One of them left the room to invite the anxious parents into the dance studio. When everybody had shuffled in, Anna Popova turned to them and the children and smiled.

"We've been very impressed with what we've seen this morning," she said. "There are many children here today who show real talent and dedication. Unfortunately, we cannot take all of them at the Imperial. This is our fourth audition and we have seen many gifted children at them all. In a minute, I'm going to read out the names of the children we would like to stay on for this afternoon's session. I'm afraid that will mean that most of you are going to be disappointed. But if you are disappointed this time round that doesn't necessarily mean that you don't have a future at the Imperial. All of you are young and there will be another opportunity for you to apply when you are in Year Six. Not succeeding this time does not necessarily mean that you won't be successful in the future. Indeed we look very favourably on reapplications, and it may be that we feel you have enormous talent but are not quite ready for the move away from home that coming to the school would entail. So if your name is not called, don't think it is the end of the road for you, but go away and work hard."

She paused. The air was thick with tension. Esme had her eyes squeezed tight shut. One of the mothers looked as if she was praying, another kept blinking very fast.

"These are the girls we would like to see this afternoon: Meredith, Violet, Alicia, Esme and Aisling. If they'd like to wait here for a few minutes, we'll take you and your parents to somewhere where you can eat your packed lunches, but of course you are free to leave the building as long as you are back by 2pm. To the rest of you, I want to say thank you and good luck with your futures, which I'm sure will be bright."

Several girls had burst into tears, either through joy or disappointment, and one mother whose daughter hadn't made it through to the afternoon session was crying, too. Anna Popova stayed in the room, but the teachers and the registrar, obviously experienced at dealing with this situation, began herding the disappointed children and parents towards the changing rooms, deftly fielding questions as they went.

Eel stood up in a daze. She felt as if someone had put a heavy stone in her stomach. She had dared to hope that she might get through to the afternoon session, but she hadn't. Her name hadn't been read out. So now she knew. She wasn't good enough. Her legs felt a bit shaky as she walked towards the door.

"Alicia! Where are you going?" called Anna Popova. "Alicia! Alicia Marvell!"

Eel swung around, suddenly aware that she was being called.

Anna Popova was smiling at her. "Didn't you hear me read your name out? You're through to the afternoon, Alicia."

Eel shook her head, and then her face lit up. "Oh, that was me," she said wonderingly. "I just didn't recognise Alicia as being me," she added.

"What are you normally called?" asked Anna Popova, kindly.

"Eel."

The teacher looked amused. "Eel! That's a first. I don't think there's ever been a ballerina called Eel before."

Eel sat quietly in the small room where Esme and her dad were eating sandwiches. Esme's mum was engrossed in reading the paper. Most of the other families had gone out to get some lunch at a local café, but Eel didn't have any money and in her rush this morning she hadn't thought to make a packed lunch. Her stomach rumbled. Esme kept glancing at Eel from under her eyelashes, and after a few minutes she edged down the bench towards her and held out a packet of cheese and cucumber sandwiches.

"Have one," said Esme.

Eel felt she should refuse but she was ravenous. "Are you sure? Have you got enough?"

"We've got piles," said Esme. "We made loads for the coach."

"The coach?" asked Eel.

"We came down from Leeds this morning, and we'll catch the coach back later today. You need loads of sandwiches because it takes for ever."

"The train would have been quicker," said Eel.

Esme nodded. "It would, but it costs a lot more than the coach."

"Oh," said Eel, feeling chastened. She hadn't thought of that. "So you must have been up for hours?"

"Yes," said Esme. "It was still dark when we left. But I don't feel tired. I'm too hyped up."

"You're very good," said Eel, taking another sandwich that Esme was pressing upon her.

"But will I be good enough?" said Esme fiercely. She sighed. "It's so hard to know. I wish I could have seen all the other auditions on the other days, then maybe I'd have a better idea. Have you been doing ballet long?"

Eel shook her head. "I'd never had dance lessons at all until last September. So just over a year."

"A year!?" Esme's voice betrayed her astonishment. "Are you sure? Only a year? That's totally amazing. No one would ever have guessed." She looked pensive. "If you've got this good in a year, just think how good you'll be when you've been doing it for ever like me."

"When did you start?" asked Eel.

"I went to baby ballet when I was three and I've been having lessons since then," said Esme. "I thought I was going to have to stop when my dad lost his job two years ago, but I was lucky, my teacher said she would teach me for free."

"If she did that you must know for certain you're good," said Eel.

"Maybe," said Esme. "The question

remains, am I good enough?"

"That's what I want to know, too," said Eel. "I thought that if I got accepted here, then I'd know."

Esme gave a tight little smile. "I've got to do more than be accepted," she said with intensity, and Eel was about to ask her what she meant when Esme's mum asked if they'd like her to take them to the park nearby where there were some swings.

"As long," she said, "as you both promise me you won't break an arm or a leg. I'd never forgive myself."

"We promise!" chorused the girls.

After she and Esme came back from the swings, the rest of the afternoon passed in a blur for Eel. All the girls took part in another class and then Eel, Esme and Violet were separated from the others and sent to see the physiotherapist. After that, Anna Popova ushered them to the door and told the three of them that they would be sent a letter in the post very soon. Eel and Esme stood on the steps of the Imperial exchanging phone numbers.

"I hope we both get in," said Eel. "It would

be fun to come here together."

"It would be a big move for me," said Esme. "I'd have to leave Yorkshire and move to London. I'd miss my home."

At the word "home" a picture of Eel's bedroom popped into her head. She suddenly realised what getting into the Imperial would mean. Her heart lurched.

"Do you think you could bear it? Leaving home, I mean," she asked Esme.

Esme looked at her, surprised. "Of course. Coming to the Imperial is what I want most in the world. I'd give up everything to come here. I'm never going to be a ballerina if I stay at home. You have to make sacrifices for ballet."

"Yes," said Eel in a small voice. "I guess you do. I just don't think I'd thought it through."

Chapter Fifteen

Olivia walked up to the door of the music room. It was ajar. Kasha's songwriting workshop had just finished. She had met some of the other participants walking down the corridor, clutching the CDs that they were going to send off for the competition. Those the judges liked most would be invited to take part in a public sing-off at the Cavendish Hall.

Olivia paused at the door. She could hear Aeysha singing. Her voice wasn't the strongest in the world, but the song was beautiful. It had a chorus with a catch in it that made Olivia's insides feel a bit funny. She waited outside the door, not wanting to disturb Aeysha and Kasha.

"That was beautiful, Aeysha," said Kasha. "I love it."

"Ah," said Aeysha, "but it was pretty ordinary until you changed those notes in the chorus. That catch has transformed it. You helped me make it something much more than it was."

"It's your song, Aeysha. All I did was make a tiny suggestion. I've been thinking, maybe you should enter this one for the competition?"

"I've been wondering that as well," said Aeysha. "But I think I'll stick with the two I'd decided on. If I'm lucky enough to get through to the live final, I'd be happier singing one of those because I've had loads of time to practise. This is brand new and I might not be so confident singing it. I'm definitely a better songwriter than I am a singer, so I think it's best to stick with those other songs."

"Your call, Aeysha," said Kasha. "But it's a great song. I'm impressed. Maybe we can work on it again together once the competition's over. I really think it's got possibilities."

"That would be lovely," Aeysha was saying as Olivia popped her head round the door.

"Are you two finished?" she asked. "I wondered whether either of you wanted to pop down to the river and see Dad."

"Love to," said Aeysha, "but I can't, I've got an English essay to finish over lunch break."

"Me neither," said Kasha. He sighed loudly. "I'm due in the recording studio. I can't say I'm looking forward to it." He looked really sad.

"Have you managed to write a song?" asked Olivia curiously.

"Yes," said Kasha, sounding pained, "but I know it's rubbish. It's not nearly as good as Aeysha's song. That's in a different league."

"You can have mine if you like," laughed Aeysha. "After all, it wouldn't be half as good without your contribution. I'll give it to you."

"No, Aeysha. That's really generous of you. But it's your song. It belongs to you. I couldn't take it."

Olivia and Kasha walked to the entrance to the Swan together, where Kasha got out his cap, pulled it down over his head and put on a pair of dark glasses.

Olivia laughed. "You draw far more attention to yourself looking like that than if you just walked down the street as yourself."

"You don't know what it's like," said Kasha gloomily. "It's not funny being chased by loads of twelve-year-olds."

"Goes with the territory," said Olivia unsympathetically. "You'd be nowhere without them."

"I know, I know," said Kasha. "Lots of people would envy me my position, and I know I owe to it to the people who buy my music." He looked pensive. "But being a pop star just isn't as much fun as I imagined it would be."

"Nobody's forcing you to do it," said Olivia quietly.

Kasha burst out laughing. "Olivia Marvell, you don't hold back, do you? But you're right. I've got what I always wanted and I shouldn't moan. I'm the luckiest boy in the whole world."

Chapter Sixteen

Olivia and Tom stood on the edge of Tower Bridge, shivering in the icy wind that whipped their cheeks until they turned pink. The sky was heavy and grey. The electronic screen on the riverbank said day seven.

"Phew, it's cold," said Tom. He stared at the figure of Jack who was sitting huddled on the wire like a small, unhappy gnome. The wire swung in the high wind. "But it's nothing compared with what it must be like for Jack." He looked at Olivia's intense, anxious face. "Do you think he's all right out there?"

Olivia shook her head. "I don't know. In these conditions it would take all your strength and concentration to stay on the wire, but to have done it for over a week is truly superhuman. It's really going to take its toll. The real dangers are exhaustion and hypothermia."

They saw Pablo beckoning to them and they ran over. It began to sleet heavily.

"I've just spoken to Jack. He's coming in for a ten-minute break. You can have a quick word. It'll cheer him up. He needs a boost."

He sent them off to greet Jack while he went to check that the team were at the ready with hot soup, a fresh thermos of tea, hot water bottles and dry clothes.

Jack walked along the wire towards Tom and Olivia carrying a load of waterproofs and wet bedding. Or rather he shuffled like an old man. He looked as if he was a hundred years old and every muscle and bone ached. But he smiled when he saw the children and raised a hand in greeting. It was a mistake. It coincided with a sudden vicious gust of wind and the gesture threw him off balance. For a moment, he teetered and Olivia thought that he was going to topple off the wire. Both she and Tom gasped, and she heard Pablo shout behind them, but just in time Jack recovered himself and stayed on the wire.

He grinned sheepishly and continued towards them but when he got up close, Olivia could see how pale, tired and vulnerable he looked. She couldn't tell if he was shaking or just shivering from the cold. There was a glittering, feverish look in his eyes. As he jumped down, a photographer ran forward and poked his camera directly into Jack's face and took a picture.

Pablo looked annoyed but he didn't say anything: he knew that the stunt needed as much publicity as it could get because that's what the sponsors demanded. They were delighted by the ongoing rivalry between Jack and Viktor, as it ensured continuing and maximum media interest.

Pablo looked after the man who was now walking briskly away. It was odd, he didn't recognise him. He certainly wasn't one of the accredited photographers, as he knew all of them by sight. He tutted and made a mental note to increase the immediate security around the end of the wire. They had somebody keeping watch both day and night to make sure nobody attempted to get up on the wire, but it couldn't hurt to be more vigilant. Only yesterday they had had to deal with a group of drunken louts who had stood on Tower Bridge at midnight taunting Jack and throwing apples at him as if

Jack was a living coconut shy there exclusively for their enjoyment. Fortunately there had been no direct hits.

Pablo looked at his stopwatch. There were only eight minutes before Jack had to be back on the wire or he would have broken the rules and Viktor would be the winner.

Olivia hugged Jack under the shelter of the little tent while the rest of the team made ready all the provisions and equipment that he would need for his return trip along the wire.

"Are you all right, Dad?" she asked anxiously.

"Fine, chick, just a little tired," he said with a smile, before he broke into a hacking cough. "My chest hurts a bit. I've got a bad cold. It's tough out there. But I comfort myself with the thought that if I'm finding it tough, then Viktor must be really struggling."

"Yes, but Viktor doesn't have a chest infection," said Olivia.

"No," said Pablo with a grin. "He's got something far worse: bad balance." The others looked at him expectantly. Pablo seemed remarkably happy given that Jack clearly wasn't in the best of shape.

"I've just heard from a friend of mine who has been down at Waterloo Bridge. Viktor has fallen off the wire twice during the last four hours, and only just managed to get back on. It's a sign that he's in a really weakened state. You're going to beat him, Jack."

But Jack said nothing because he was caught by another spasm of coughing. Pablo looked worried. "I think we'd better get a doctor down here during your next break to have a listen to your chest." He turned to Olivia and Tom. "Probably best not to go round broadcasting to everyone that Jack's sick. We don't want it to get out in the media. Wouldn't be good for morale. Viktor's team might find a way to capitalise on it."

"Dad," said Olivia slowly, "if you *are* sick, there would be no shame in giving up."

Jack looked at her aghast as he walked back towards the wire. "Give up?" he said. "Never!" He suddenly brightened. "I'll only be coming off the wire after thirty days." He saluted as he stepped out on to the wire and the wind howled as if in welcome.

"He's impossible," said Olivia, sighing.

"But if it was you out there, you'd never

give up either, would you, Liv?" said Tom, seriously.

"Probably not," conceded Olivia.

Tom laughed. "Like father, like daughter," he said.

Olivia turned to Pablo. "So your friend, the one who knows about Viktor falling off the wire, is he a kind of spy?"

"Not really, he's just doing me a favour and reporting back on how Viktor is faring, seeing if he can pick up any gossip from the journalists or the team." He saw Olivia's face. "No dirty tricks, I promise. You know that's not our style. But knowing what is going on in the other camp can give you a psychological advantage in an endurance stunt like this. Success or failure is so much in the mind."

"But if you're checking out his camp," said Tom slowly, "then it probably means that people are checking out ours."

Pablo nodded. "What do they say? All's fair in love and war. Well, this is a kind of war. There can only be one Viktor. That's why you need to be careful what you say. Only talk about how Jack's getting along and his state of health to the people you *really* trust."

Chapter Seventeen

Olivia, Tom and the others stared in shock at the double-page spread in the *Comet*, a tabloid newspaper, that lay open on the table in front of them. In the centre were two large pictures of Jack. In one, he looked happy and smiling and boyish, and in the other he looked haggard, ill and ancient. Olivia could tell from the angle that it had been snatched by the unknown photographer as Jack had stumbled off the wire when she and Tom had been down at the bridge.

Across the top of the pages was a big headline in bold black letters that read: *High-Wire Walker Hits Rock Bottom*. The story went on to say that the world-renowned Jack Marvell was feeling the pressure in his head-to-head with ace stuntman Viktor and that the stress was making him ill. It looked likely that he would concede defeat to the Russian within the next few days.

Tom read out the rest of the story: " 'Sources close to the Marvell camp say that the Great Marvello has been suffering from bronchitis and, combined with the appalling weather conditions on the wire over the last few days, this has brought the daredevil to his knees. 'He's a finished man,' said the source. 'It's only a matter of time.' Pablo Catalano, a spokesman for Marvell, was tight-lipped but confirmed that the high-wire walker had been suffering from a bad cold, but he insisted that there were no plans to cut short the world-record attempt. 'Jack Marvell is in it for the duration.'"

Tom took a deep breath and continued: " 'He would say that,' said Viktor, during one of his ten-minute comfort breaks. 'We've heard that the marvellous Marvell is close to breaking point. I've never felt better in my life. I could probably manage sixty days on the high wire.'"

There was a short silence when Tom finished. Eel took a great gulp of air and looked as if she was struggling not to cry, while Tom looked anxiously at Olivia as she gnawed the knuckle on her right hand.

"But it's all rubbish!" said Aeysha. "Everyone will know that it is, and even if they don't, as long as Jack doesn't see the newspaper report, it doesn't really matter. The only damage it can do is psychological, if he's feeling a bit down and ill. But if he doesn't see it, it doesn't really matter what the newspapers are saying, does it? And Pablo is smart enough to make sure he doesn't know anything about it."

"Aeysha's right," said Georgia brightly. "He need never know."

But when they all trooped down to the river a little later, there were masses of TV crews down on the banks and a crowd had gathered. Some were shouting their support but there was a gaggle on the bridge yelling, "Give up! Give up! It's all over, Marvell!" Olivia wondered if they had been paid to be there.

The Swans stood on the bank, looking horrified. Just when it didn't seem as if things could get worse, they did. A light aircraft with Viktor's sponsor's name on it started circling above where Jack was perched in the drizzle. Behind it flowed a banner on which was written: *"Jack Marvell staring defeat in the face!"* Olivia saw her dad stare up at the sky for a long time, then drop his head.

Pablo had come to join them. "This," he said, through gritted teeth, "is all-out psychological warfare."

"I could kill the rat who's been leaking stuff to the papers," said Olivia fiercely, "they deserve a long, slow, lingering death." Eel burst into tears.

Olivia looked at her little sister in surprise. She wasn't normally so sensitive. "It's all right, Eel, I'm not really going to kill anyone! Yet..."

Chapter Eighteen

Alex and Eel were alone in one of the music rooms.

Eel's face was red with anger. "It had to have been you, Alex Parks!" she cried. "You are the only other person who knew that Jack was ill. None of the others would dream of giving away any information about Jack's stunt. They're too loyal to do something so nasty. I would never have told you if I'd realised that you were going to use the information in such a terrible way. I only mentioned it because you seemed so interested in Jack's stunt and so admiring of what he's doing. I thought you were on his side. I thought you could be trusted."

Alex smiled at her patronisingly. "You're jumping to conclusions, Eel," he said. "Of course it wasn't me. Who would I tell, anyway? I don't have any interest in who wins some silly high-wire competition. It could have been anyone. If you knew, lots of people must have known."

Eel considered this. Perhaps he was right? She'd been eaten up with guilt since the piece about Jack had been published, convinced that it was her babbling to Alex that had done the damage. He had seemed so genuinely interested in what Jack was doing. But it was true, lots of people talked carelessly, and maybe she was being unfair in accusing him like this.

"OK," she conceded. "Maybe I was wrong. I'm just so worried about my dad. I'm sorry."

"Apology accepted," said Alex, with a smirk. "It could have been one of his team, or one of Livy's friends. They're always in the café across the road, gossiping and talking about each other. Georgia's got a big mouth. She probably let something slip and it was overheard by a journalist or something."

"Don't talk about Georgia like that!" said Eel, hotly. "Everyone loves Georgia, and she really likes you."

Alex raised an eyebrow. "Georgia! I'm out of her league, and anyway I'll talk how I like.

You still owe me, Eel Marvell."

There was an edge to Alex's voice that Eel didn't like. She wished that she'd never got Alex involved in her secret scheme to audition at the Imperial. She'd been taken in by his lazy smile and open admiration for Olivia. But now it felt as if he had some kind of hold over her. Still, she wasn't going to let him see that she was rattled.

"Look, Alex," she said as sweetly as she could. "I did what I promised I would. I tried to put in a good word for you with Livy, but it was a complete waste of time. She so clearly wasn't interested in you."

Eel didn't say it out loud but inside she was thinking what a good thing it was, too. Alex clearly wasn't half as nice as he made out. Or maybe his pride was just so dented by Olivia's disdain that he'd become some kind of monster.

Livy had briefly confided in Eel what had happened between her and Alex and sworn Eel to secrecy.

"I tried to let him down gently, Eel," she'd said. "But I think I made a terrible hash of it. I can still feel him looking at me, but his gaze is cold and hostile. I wish he'd stop coming to high-wire but it's like he's trying to prove something.

I was loving *Dream* rehearsals but now they feel spoiled. I wish Tom was playing Demetrius and wasn't just the understudy."

Eel had tried to soothe her sister, but she could see why a boy like Alex might find it hard to be turned down by a girl he was keen on. In fact, she had the evidence in front of her eyes. The Alex in front of her now didn't seem anything like the Alex who'd been so eager to help her try out for the Imperial.

"Of course, I could let your gran know what you've been up to?" said Alex softly.

Eel's stomach did a somersault, but she wasn't going to let Alex see how worried she was.

"You could," she said, trying to sound completely unfazed, "but of course if you did, you'd be in as much trouble as me."

Alex shot her a look of fury and spun on his heel. At the door, he turned back and snarled: "You stuck-up Marvell sisters deserve everything you get!"

Eel waited until she was certain that he was too far away to hear and then she burst into noisy sobs. She wished she could turn back the clock to before she'd even thought of applying for the Imperial, before she'd got involved with Alex and before she'd got herself into this terrible mess.

Suddenly, Aeysha popped her head round the door.

"Eel," she said, both surprised and concerned to find her crying. Eel was normally such a cheerful little soul. She put her arms around the younger girl. "Is it anything I can help with?" she asked gently.

Eel looked up at Aeysha, her face wet with tears. "Aeysha, have you ever done anything you really regret?"

"Loads of times," said Aeysha. "There was the time I told my brother that I hated him and so did all my brothers and sisters, and he went out on his bicycle and fell off and gashed his forehead, and for days after I was consumed by guilt because I was convinced that I had caused the accident, when in fact there was something wrong with the peddle on his bike and it would have happened anyway. But it didn't make me feel any less bad. I knew that I should never have said what I did. He's still got the scar on his forehead and I still feel a little twinge of guilt every time I see it. But my brother just laughed.

He loves me, so he could forgive me."

"That's quite bad," said Eel. "But I think I've been badder, and it's got really complicated."

"Well," said Aeysha, "the best thing would be to come clean. Most things can be put right if you talk about them. Keeping secrets makes things fester. Do you want to tell me about it?"

"I'll think about it," said Eel, wiping her tears.

"Well, anytime," said Aeysha.

Eel sighed. "At least Livy told Alex Parks where to get off," she said.

"I guessed as much," said Aeysha.

Eel clapped her hand over her mouth. "Oh, didn't she tell you?"

Aeysha smiled. "You know Livy, she's like an oyster."

"I'm pleased she did," said Eel, as the bell rang for afternoon lessons. "I don't think he's a very nice person at all."

Chapter Nineteen

Alicia and India Taylor were in Alicia's office, drinking tea.

"Something's wrong," said Alicia. "She's stopped taking extra classes in jazz and tap, and when she is there, Mrs Merman says that her work has tailed right off."

"The same in ballet," said India. "It's so odd, at the beginning of the term Eel was making extraordinary progress. And I do mean *extraordinary*. You could actually see improvements from lesson to lesson. It was as if she was inspired. But now she seems listless and distracted. You don't think she's worried about her dad, do you?"

"Well, both of them do worry about him, of course. We all do. It can't be easy having Jack as your father. He's away such a lot, what he does is dangerous and his successes and failures are so very public. This latest stunt is particularly gruelling, and it's worse for the girls because it's being so closely documented by the press. I know it's stressful for him, but I'm not sure he ever considered how stressful it would be for those of us watching him. I can't wait for it to be over."

India smiled to herself. Alicia's relationship with her son-in-law was often difficult but she had clearly developed a strong affection for him in the year or so since he had turned up destitute at the Swan with Olivia and Eel in tow.

"But I think it's something more than Jack that is worrying her," said Alicia.

"I do wonder whether we should have put her forward to audition for the Imperial," said India.

"I've wondered that, too. Jack and I talked about it and we decided against, but of course he was strongly guided by me. Now I feel that perhaps it was a mistake. Maybe it would have answered some of the questions she was asking about her own talent."

"Have you tried talking to her?"

"Tried and failed," said Alicia. 'She's not called Eel for nothing. She can be a slippery little thing."

"You could perhaps speak to the Imperial. You know Anna Popova personally, don't you?"

"But the deadline for applying is long gone and I'm sure the auditions will be over," said Alicia.

"Probably, but Anna might be prepared just to look at her. As a favour to you."

"I would feel compromised even asking," said Alicia.

"I understand," said India. "And it's your call. But…" She paused.

"But what?" asked Alicia.

"It would be terrible to see Eel's talent wither and die."

After India had gone, Alicia stared out of the window for a long time, her colleague's words running through her mind.

Georgia put away her music and closed the piano lid. She had done quite enough practice for one day and she still had several weeks before her piano exam. She looked at the clock on her phone. If she hurried, she would have time to spend a few minutes with Katie and the others before afternoon school began. Katie was going to Yorkshire tomorrow to film her TV series and she wanted to make sure she said goodbye.

Georgia had just put her music into her bag when the door opened and Alex walked in. Georgia was so flustered that she dropped her bag and everything spilled out of it. She turned bright red as a smelly pair of socks she used for jazz class, a half-eaten apple, her hairbrush covered in blonde hairs, four bottles of nail varnish and two biros with badly-chewed ends dropped at his feet. But Alex didn't seem to mind. He bent down to help her retrieve the items and gave her a devastating smile as he handed her the biros and their hands brushed. Georgia smiled nervously back and her insides felt as if they had melted.

"I'm glad I found you, Georgie," said Alex. "I've been wanting to talk to you alone for ages."

Georgia blinked and tried to look cool. Olivia hadn't said anything, but Georgia was certain that something had happened between her and Alex. There was an atmosphere between them in high-wire lessons and the *Dream* rehearsals were full of tension. She'd heard a rumour flying around the school that Olivia had asked Alex out and he had laughed in her face, but when she had found a way to casually mention this to Aeysha, in the hope she could fill her in on the details, her friend had looked at her as if she was mad and said: "You can believe what you like, Georgia, but I'd put money on it that the source of that rumour is Alex Parks himself."

Then she had added more gently: "Forget him, Georgia. He's almost certainly trouble. Set your sights on someone nice. Like Connor. He's been mad about you ever since you played Cinderella."

Georgia had bristled and snapped, "When I want romantic advice, I'll ask for it Aeysha, thank you," and things had been a bit tense between them for a couple of days. But Aeysha's unfailing good nature made it hard to be angry with her for long, and Georgia had soon thawed.

Georgia had noticed that Alex stared at Olivia as much as ever but he no longer had that puppy dog look in his eyes that she found so appealing. It was more as if he was appraising Olivia for some other purpose. She tried to remember Aeysha's warning words, but Alex's close proximity made her forget everything except that he was undoubtedly the most beautiful boy she had ever seen.

"Georgia," he said softly, and his voice was like syrup falling off a spoon. "I really like you, Georgia." He paused.

Georgia didn't know what to say, and was horrified to hear her own voice squeaking like Minnie Mouse: "Really?"

"Yes, really," said Alex gently. "I want to ask you out." He looked very shy, as if she would be doing him a great honour.

"Me?" breathed Georgia. "You want to go out with me? Just you and me? On our own? Just us?" Georgia realised she was babbling.

"Yes, just you and me. Together," said Alex. He grinned. "I'll even pay."

Georgia felt confused. She had dreamed of this moment and wanted to think that she was the chosen one after all, but she wasn't a fool. She had witnessed too many of Alex's lingering looks at Olivia and his complete indifference to her in the past. She needed to ask him about Olivia, but hardly dared.

"And ... Livy?" she stuttered.

Alex gave an amused grin. "Ancient history." He took a step nearer. "I've been a fool, Georgie, but I've had my eyes opened. You've been there all along, right under my nose, and I was so stupid that I didn't notice before. But now I have. You're the one."

Georgia felt as if all her bones had magically been transformed into feathers.

"So will you come out with me, Georgie?"

Georgia realised that Alex was still holding her smelly socks. She turned crimson with embarrassment, grabbed them out of his hand and blurted: "Yes, please."

Alex flashed his irresistible smile. "Good." He ambled towards the door, where he stopped and turned. "For the time being, let's just keep this between you and me, shall we? We don't want to be fodder for the gossips, do we?"

Georgia nodded. "I'd hate that."

"Me too," smiled Alex, and then he was gone. Georgia stood for a moment, staring after him, and then she slid down the wall with shock and excitement, absentmindedly stuffing her dirty socks into her mouth. It was a second or two before she realised what she had done and spat them out again.

Chapter Twenty

There was a big crowd down at the river. It was a blustery day with a chill in the air, but the winter sun was trying to peep out from behind the clouds. The electronic board announced that it was day fourteen of the river challenge. Both men were almost halfway through. Olivia, Eel and the others were watching Jack on the wire. He was walking up and down it on his hands. The crowd roared their approval. He flipped back on to his feet and doffed his cap to the audience. Then he took five balls out of his coat pocket and began to juggle with them. The crowd clapped wildly.

Lots of people were taking videos that would soon find their way on to YouTube. The onlookers always liked it best when Jack was most active. During the three tense days when Jack's chest infection seemed to have the better of him, the crowd had drifted away, and people had complained on social networking sites that Jack Marvell was boring, and that Viktor Ivanov was offering much better entertainment by Waterloo Bridge. But Jack was well and truly wooing them back. After he finished the juggling, he balanced a board on the wire and proceeded to crack eggs into a bowl and whisk them.

"What's he doing?" asked Tom, puzzled.

Olivia shrugged. "I don't know," she said, watching him add flour and milk to the eggs.

"Maybe he's baking a cake," said Eel.

"I don't think so," said Aeysha. "He can't possibly have an oven out there."

The crowd was intrigued, too, wondering what Jack was up to. He set up a little gas-burner on the board, put a small frying pan on top and poured in a little of the mixture.

"Of course!" exclaimed Georgia. "It's Shrove Tuesday. He's making pancakes!" She smiled at Olivia and said: "Your dad, he's so clever. What a brilliant thing to do."

Olivia grinned back at Georgia. Her friend had seemed so much happier during the last few days, and all the snippiness seemed to have entirely disappeared. Clearly telling Alex she wasn't interested in him had been the right thing for Olivia to do. She only wished she had noticed and done something about it earlier. She hated to think she had done anything to make Georgia unhappy, however unwittingly. Her friends were more important to her than Alex Parks' feelings.

Jack was now clowning around and tossing pancakes high up into the air. To the delight of the crowd, he started throwing them down to the police in the river launch that was circling under the wire, and to a group of press photographers in a motor boat.

"This is more like it," said Pablo, happily. "Your dad is back on top form. I have to admit there were a couple of days when I was really worried. Not just about his chest but about his state of mind, too. It's lonely out there on the wire, day after day, hour after hour. You need the crowd to help you."

"But there was no real possibility of him giving up, was there?" asked Tom.

"Well, after that stuff in the papers it was touch and go," said Pablo. "It's clear that Viktor's strategy, or rather his manager's strategy, is to psych Jack out, and he almost succeeded."

"But maybe," said Olivia slowly, "that means that Ethan Rees doesn't think much of Viktor's staying power."

Pablo grinned. "That's exactly what I think." He tapped the side of his nose and said, "Anyway, we've got a trick or two up our sleeve."

"But they're not dirty tricks?" asked Aeysha.

"No, course not," said Pablo, quickly. "Just more where the pancakes came from."

"Tell us," said Eel excitedly.

"Be patient," said Pablo. "Your dad is coming in for ten minutes very soon. He can tell you all."

Eel was sitting on Jack's knee, playing with his hair.

"You really are better?" asked Olivia, anxiously.

"Never fitter," said Jack, with a grin. "I had a little wobble, but it's passed. I'm good."

"I'm sorry, Dad," said Eel, looking stricken.

He smiled at her, puzzled. "Don't be sorry, Eel, it wasn't your fault that the Viktor camp managed to get a tidbit of information about my state of health to use to his advantage. It's just a reminder that we have to be really careful about letting information out of the camp. We need to play our cards close to our chest."

"So does that mean you can't tell us about the big stunt you've got planned for Friday night?" asked Tom.

Jack smiled. "I can risk it. You are Livy and Eel's friends, and I know you are all completely trustworthy. Besides, in this instance we actually need you to spread the word. We need to encourage people to come down here at 9pm on Friday with the promise that something amazing is going to happen. We won't tell people what it is, but we will try and pique their interest. We want a big crowd so we can really give them a good show."

"But what are you going to do?" asked everyone, excitedly.

Jack leaned forward to whisper. "I'm going to give them a firework display. I'm going to create a river of fire across the wire. Things are really going to go with a bang. That's the big secret."

Chapter Twenty-One

Kasha stopped strumming his battered guitar and looked miserably at the gaggle of people gathered in the corner of the recording studio. Lucie Groves was speaking very fast to the producer and another record-company executive. He knew that they were discussing him and his feeble effort of a song, and to be honest he wasn't surprised. It wasn't good enough. He was really proud of the two singles he'd already released and the rest of the album, but this song was just like a thousand other fluffy pop songs. It was cotton wool for the brain. The group broke up and Lucie Groves came and sat down by him. Kasha couldn't look her in the eye.

"Kasha, I think you know as well as I do

that 'Bruised' just isn't good enough. You have so much talent, talent that we've put a lot of investment into, so it's in no one's interest to put out a product that's less than first class. Every song on the album has got to be a potential hit otherwise the press will be all over you. They'll say you're just another pretty face designed to separate teenage girls from their money; not the real deal – a proper singer-songwriter.

"We want you to have a broader appeal than just the teenage market. We want you to take them with you as they grow older like the really big stars do. We signed you because we thought you would have longevity, Kasha, and this song ... this song, well, it's just ... just..."

"...just not good enough." Kasha finished the sentence for her.

"The thing is," continued Lucie, "the sort of investment we're making in you means that we're expecting a long-term return, and that means that you've got to deliver, and deliver every time." She paused and looked him straight in the eye. "If you can't hack it, then we might have to rethink that investment."

Kasha wished Lucie would stop using the word "investment"; it made him feel as if he were a prize pig being fattened up until the moment he could be turned into bacon.

"Listen," said Lucie, "all I'm asking is that you come up with something distinctive. That's the point about all your other stuff, it's so original, it sounds like you and no one else. That's what we want, Kasha, and I'm afraid we need it now…"

Lucie shook her head sorrowfully. The threat was left hanging in the air. Kasha knew that they wouldn't just cut him loose immediately. The record company had too much at stake. The album was announced and the tour was already sold out. They had spent too much money to just drop him. But he knew what would happen. Unless the first album went straight to number one and was a massive hit, they would turn their attention to someone else. You only got one chance in this business at being the next big thing, and he could see his slipping through his fingers. He thought about just standing up with his guitar and walking out the door. But he knew that would be stupid. He had dreamed all his life of being a pop star.

"Listen, Kasha," said Lucie, "I'm just going to pop out and get myself and the guys a coffee, and maybe you could play around with the song for a bit. I'll bring you back a double espresso to pep you up."

She went to get her coat and bag, and stopped to talk to the others. Kasha strummed his guitar moodily. A melody floated into his head. He tried it out, and then played it again. He smiled to himself, a little despairing. He knew why he liked it so much. It was almost exactly the same as the chorus that Aeysha had played to him in her song this morning. He had just given yet another little tweak to the catch. He played it again, totally absorbed. It really was very good and totally distinctive. He strummed it one more time. He looked up to see Lucie and the others staring at him, a look of real excitement on their faces.

"Don't stop, Kasha," said Lucie excitedly. "That's fantastic. It's just what we need. Splice it in with the other stuff you wrote and suddenly 'Bruised' is transformed. It's a winner. We might even be able to release it as a single."

"But…" said Kasha.

"I won't hear any 'buts'," said Lucie imperiously.

"The thing is…" began Kasha.

"The thing is we need to lay this track down," said Lucie firmly. "Every minute in here is costing us money."

She nodded to the band, who had taken their places and were already playing variations on the tune Kasha had been strumming.

"Look," said Kasha, "it's not really all my…"

"Look," said Lucie speaking over him, "let's get to work." She kissed Kasha on the cheek. "Come on, golden boy, let's make you a superstar."

Kasha hesitated. All he had to do was admit that the bit of the song they liked so much belonged to Aeysha, not to him. But he could see that Lucie was not in the mood for any complications. In any case, he reasoned, most of the song was his. It was just that tiny bit that was hers. And it was his tweak that had made it really stand out. Besides, nobody would ever know. Aeysha wouldn't even notice. Lots of bits of songs sounded like other songs. And nobody was really going to hear Aeysha's song. She'd said she wasn't going to enter it for the songwriting competition, so he might be the only other person in the world who'd heard it.

He'd ring her and explain. He saw the others looking at him impatiently.

"OK," he said, "let's do it." And right at that moment, he felt as if a little bit of him deep inside had withered and died.

Chapter Twenty-Two

Aeysha stood in the classroom on her own with an envelope and three CDs in her hand. She had already put her application form for the song contest in the envelope. All she had to do now was add her CDs, seal it and take it to Mrs Gibbs to post.

She put the CDs on a desk and stared at them. She had told Kasha that she was going to enter the first two songs she'd written and recorded for the competition, but now that the deadline was fast approaching, she wasn't so sure. Kasha had told her how much he liked the third song she had composed in the final workshop and Aeysha really valued his opinion. He knew what he was talking about.

She picked up the CD with that particular

song on it, the one that he had transformed by making that small but crucial change to the catch in the chorus. No, she was much better to stick to the two songs that she had really practised singing. She put down the CD and pushed the other two into the envelope, sealed it with tape, and headed out of the door, shutting it behind her.

A few seconds later the door to the classroom opened and Aeysha reappeared. She walked over to the desk, slit the envelope with a scalpel and shook out the two CDs. The three CDs sat side by side on the desk. For a moment her hand hovered over all three of them, a look of indecision on her face. Then she scooped two of them into the envelope and resealed it. She walked down the corridor to the hatch in reception where she found Eel asking Mrs Gibbs if any post had come for Jack.

"No, Eel, nothing today," said Mrs Gibbs. She watched Eel walk away and smiled fondly. "It's sweet the way she's so concerned for her dad's post. I think it's her way of looking after him when he's out there in all weathers." She turned to Aeysha. "What can I do for you, young lady?"

Aeysha held up the envelope. "It's my entry for the songwriting competition."

"I'll put it with the others," said Mrs Gibbs with a smile. "I'm going to send them all off tonight. I heard you've got a real talent for it, Aeysha. Maybe you'll win."

"Maybe pigs will fly," said Aeysha, with a grin. "It's an open contest. There might be people who've written songs professionally. I doubt I'll even get through to the next round."

"Well, good luck," said Mrs Gibbs.

Aeysha walked through the school, looking for Georgia. She'd been very elusive recently. Aeysha was pleased that her friend seemed so much happier. In fact, as Tom had remarked only that morning, Georgia didn't just seem happier, she was positively glowing. It was as if she were lit from inside by a candle. She seemed to have stopped hankering after Alex and throwing him longing looks, too. Maybe Georgia had at last got over her crush? Aeysha wasn't sorry. She thought Georgia had had a lucky escape.

In the distance, Aeysha saw Tom heading up the stairs towards the classrooms, and she was about to follow him when her mobile rang.

It was her mum. Aeysha settled herself down on the bottom step. Telephone conversations with her mum were never brief.

When Tom reached the top of the stairs, he saw that the door that led on to the lower roof was ajar. He couldn't imagine that anybody would be out there in this weather, which was dry but really chilly. He went to pull the door shut when he heard voices. He recognised them at once as belonging to Georgia and Alex. What on earth were they doing on the roof?

Tom was about to step through the door when he heard Alex say: "Right. You go down first and I'll follow in a couple of minutes."

Then Georgia said: "Alex, I don't like all this creeping around. Why don't we just go down together. What does it matter if we're seen?"

"Look babe," said Alex, his voice soft and buttery. "I just don't want Liv to be hurt after I rejected her to be with you, and I certainly don't want to do anything to destroy your friendship with her and the others. So let's just take it nice and slow. In a while, when things settle down, we can be together openly in the school, but at the moment it's best to play it cool."

Tom frowned. He had an urge to crash through the door and confront Alex. It was obvious that he was talking rubbish about Liv. He had heard the rumour flying round the school, but he didn't believe a word of it and he desperately wanted to set Georgia straight. But it would be too embarrassing to be caught eavesdropping.

Besides, although he didn't like Alex Parks, he was pleased for Georgia. She had been hankering after Alex since the very first day of term. Well, now it looked as if she had got what she wanted. If she wanted to go about with Alex Parks, it was her business. Besides, Tom was really rather pleased that Alex had turned his attentions elsewhere. It meant that he wouldn't be bothering Liv any more. Tom would never admit it to anyone, but he had been really jealous of Alex's good looks and confident manner and if Alex and Liv had gone out together he knew that he wouldn't have been happy about it one little bit.

"OK," said Georgia, but Tom could hear the reluctance in her voice. "But will I see you tonight?"

"Oh, I'll be there," said Alex. "I wouldn't

want to miss Jack Marvell's triumph for the world."

Was there something odd in his tone, thought Tom as he slipped away, or was it just that he couldn't stand Alex Parks? He wished Georgia had chosen someone nicer, but it wasn't his place to say anything.

Chapter Twenty-Three

It was just before eight o'clock at night. The river danced and sparkled under the lights from the bridge and the towpath. The odd flake of snow was falling, and Eel and Emmy were skipping around trying to catch them. The wind had dropped and it was a lovely London night.

Olivia hugged herself and grinned at Aeysha. She could see Georgia and Tom heading towards them, Georgia craning her neck around as if she were looking for someone.

It was a perfect night for fireworks. Word had got round that something really special was going to happen and the crowd was building. Jack had been busy since it had turned dark, setting up the display, nimbly working his way up and down the wire. Pulling it off was going to be something of a technical feat. It would have been easier to pull off during daylight hours, but that would have drawn attention to what he was planning. He wanted an element of surprise for the crowd's sake, but he also wanted to keep what he was doing under wraps from the Viktor camp.

Needless to say, the word that a secret stunt was happening at Tower Bridge at nine o'clock had reached the Waterloo team and they had announced that they would be doing something special at eight. Jack and Pablo hadn't minded in the slightest, in fact they had rubbed their hands in glee. Whatever Viktor did earlier in the evening wouldn't be nearly as spectacular as their event, and they hoped that as soon as the fireworks started, any crowds at Waterloo would drift their way too.

"I wonder what Viktor is going to do," said Tom, as the time edged towards eight o'clock.

"Well, whatever it is, it's not going to be a patch on Jack's stunt," said Olivia, happily.

"No chance," said Georgia, with a smile.

"I wouldn't be so sure," said Pablo, who had come up behind them. His face was grim.

"What's the matter?" asked Olivia.

"There's been a real flurry of activity down at Waterloo over the last hour or so. Viktor has been setting something up on the wire but it's impossible to see what it is. I just wish I knew…" He broke off as they heard a huge whoosh, a violent bang and saw the sky downriver blazing red and white and blue. Rockets streaked across the sky, turning it into a dark backdrop for flowers of silver, scarlet and gold. The crowd went crazy, and some of them began running off the bridge and down the towpath to get closer to the source of this marvellous display.

There was bang after bang. An arc of stars rose into the sky and then started to fall to earth like a fiery waterfall. Fountains of fire rose up into the air and then exploded into shimmering silver and crimson sparks, like celestial confetti. The display went on and on, with each marvellous explosion topped by one even more spectacular. Great clouds of smoke drifted across the sky as if London had been invaded by fire-breathing dragons.

Olivia and the others watched open-mouthed in disbelief. It was the best firework display that any of them had seen. Ever. She glanced towards Jack, who was standing on the wire with his head in his hands.

The display was so spectacular and so prolonged that it was almost nine o'clock by the time it finished. As the final rockets exploded they spelled out Viktor's initials in red sparks in the sky and, as the finale came to an end, it began to rain, a heavy miserable drizzle that soaked everyone to the skin.

The crowds, thrilled by what they had seen, began to put up their umbrellas, and many hurried off to the tube station. A few drifted back towards Tower Bridge. By the time the chimes of Big Ben signalled the hour, the rain had turned to great sheets and the wind had begun to gust.

Out on the wire, Jack attempted to light his first firework. It fizzled damply and promptly went out.

Chapter Twenty-Four

Olivia and the others were once again staring gloomily at a double-page spread in the *Comet*. The headline read: *Viktor's Gift to London!* and then underneath in smaller letters: *Rival's display turns into a damp squib*. There was a picture of Jack, taken with a long lens from the bridge, trying to light a firework and looking miserable.

He had eventually managed to get the display underway but it was nothing compared with Viktor's spectacular effort, and the driving rain meant that there was only a small huddle of people, mostly friends and supporters from the Swan, who stayed watching until the end. A stunt that everyone had felt certain would be a sure-fire winner now looked like a total failure. Once again Viktor had got the upper hand.

Tom squeezed Olivia's shoulder. "Your dad will bounce back. He always does."

"I expect you're right, but he looked so miserable," said Olivia, plaintively.

"It was such bad luck that Viktor had exactly the same idea," said Georgia, squeezing Olivia's hand sympathetically.

"If it *was* bad luck," said Olivia ominously. "Pablo doesn't think it was a coincidence that Viktor came up with the firework stunt. He thinks he somehow got wind of what was planned and set out to sabotage it. He thinks someone's deliberately giving Viktor's camp information. He's really worried."

"But who would do such a terrible thing?" asked Georgia.

"Sometimes people don't realise what they're doing by letting something slip," said Eel, quietly.

Aeysha suddenly looked really worried. "I did tell my mum about the fireworks when we were chatting before school," she said.

Olivia smiled. "Listen, Aeysha, I really don't think your mum is a spy for Viktor or his manager, do you?"

"No," said Aeysha, smiling, "I'd lay my

life on the line to say she wasn't. You have to trust the people you love."

"Well, from now on," said Tom, "everyone's lips must remain sealed about any of Jack's exploits or movements."

"Yes," agreed Olivia. "Pablo said we shouldn't even talk about when he'll be taking any of his breaks." A text came through on her phone. "That was Pablo to say Jack's coming off the wire shortly. I'm going down there."

"We'll all come," chorused the others.

Olivia smiled. "Thank you. I know he's really touched by all your support."

"Actually," said Aeysha, shyly, "that reminds me. I don't know if you'll want to come but I'll definitely need your support." She pulled a letter out of her pocket. "They liked my songs. I'm through to the live final of the songwriting contest!" Everyone squealed with excitement.

"Of course we'll come," said Georgia happily. "That's what friends do."

"You should tell Kasha," said Olivia. "He'll be thrilled for you."

Aeysha nodded and hugged the letter to her chest.

Chapter Twenty-Five

Aeysha just managed to squeeze on to the bus before the driver closed the doors. She'd stayed late at school to practice her song and now she just wanted to get home. There were no seats on the bottom deck so she climbed the stairs. It was pretty full up there too, and the windows of the bus had steamed up.

She gave a start as she saw Alex sitting right at the front of the bus. There was a woman with heavy shopping bags sitting beside him. Even if the seat had been free, Aeysha wouldn't have sat down next to him. He had been spreading untrue rumours about Olivia and him around the school, and as far as Aeysha could see, a surprising number of normally quite intelligent people seemed to believe him. Particularly the female ones. It was extraordinary what good looks and a winning smile could get away with.

Aeysha took a seat a couple of rows behind Alex and got out her copy of *Animal Farm*, which they were reading for English. She looked up at the sound of a mobile phone ringing. It was Alex's. Aeysha felt embarrassed to be eavesdropping, but she couldn't help it. Most of the front of the bus would be able to hear him.

Alex was making an arrangement with a friend to play football on Saturday. Then she heard him say: "A party? Tonight?"

There was a pause while the person at the other end spoke. Then Alex replied: "No, mate, I can't. I said I'd see this girl. Yes, Georgia, the one I told you about. She's pretty enough, but a bit of a pain."

Aeysha sat bolt upright and scowled at the back of Alex's head. He continued, "Yeah, I'll dump her soon. But she suits my purpose at the moment. Actually, I'm quite enjoying keeping the whole thing hush-hush. Adds a bit of spice. Otherwise it'd all just be a dreadful yawn."

There was another pause. Then he said: "Why didn't you say that Kerry was going to be there? Of course I'm coming if she's split up with Josh. You know I've always really liked her! I'll ring Georgia and come up with some excuse. She believes anything I tell her. I can twist her round my little finger."

Aeysha was beside herself with fury. She could barely contain the urge to storm up to him and confront him. But she couldn't bear to make such a public scene, and it wouldn't help Georgia.

Aeysha glared at the back of his head, hoping he might spontaneously combust right there on the top deck of the bus. It would serve him right. Then it occurred to her that if he got up to leave the bus, he'd see her sitting there and guess that she'd heard every word. She didn't want that to happen. She wanted to get to Georgia before he did.

Quickly, Aeysha stuffed her book back in her bag and got off the bus even though it was still ages until her own stop. She watched its tail-lights disappear and then began walking in the direction of home. It was too cold to hang around the bus stop waiting for the next one. Besides the walk would give her some thinking time, and Aeysha knew that she needed to think hard. How was she going to warn Georgia about what Alex was really like without causing Georgia too much pain?

"It's not true!" said Georgia. Her cheeks were red and her eyes dark and fierce. "You're making it up." She suddenly blazed. "Did Livy put you up to this? What's going on? Is she jealous that I'm the one that Alex chose in the end after he turned her down? That's what this is all about, isn't it?"

"Georgia," said Aeysha gently. "Do you really believe that Alex turned Livy down? Remember the way he used to moon over her? You can't have forgotten how unhappy it made you. If anyone did the turning down it was almost certainly Livy."

"What matters is that he's with me now," cried Georgia. "So why are you trying to spoil it by telling me he's not to be trusted? What do you know?"

Aeysha sighed heavily. This was not going well. "I told you what I overheard him saying on the bus. And anyway, why does he want to keep your friendship a secret? Seems odd to me."

"There's nothing the least bit odd about it,"

said Georgia huffily. "We just don't want people gossiping about us. You know what a hotbed the Swan is for that kind of thing. The only thing I think is odd is that you've been going round spying on Alex. I thought you were supposed to be my friend, someone who I can trust."

"Oh Georgie," said Aeysha, suddenly feeling tearful. "I *am* your friend. That's why I'm telling you this. I'm just trying to look out for you. I really care about you and don't want you to get hurt. I can't help what I heard on the bus."

"That's rubbish!" said Georgia, furiously. "You just don't want me to be happy. You can't bear to think that I don't need you and the others as much as I did because I've got Alex. But you were the one who told me when we were in Edinburgh that things change, and that change is a good thing. Well, I'm changing, and you're changing, too. Everything's going to be different at the end of this year because you're leaving the Swan. You never consulted me about that. You never considered how that would make me feel. So why are you so bothered about my feelings now? Just leave me and Alex alone and stop treating me as if I'm a stupid baby who can't look after herself."

There was a coldness in Georgia's eyes that Aeysha had never seen before. "Just answer me one question, Georgia," she said to her friend.

"What?"

"Were you supposed to see Alex last night and did he cancel on you?"

For a second, Georgia looked surprised but then she rallied and stuck out her chin defiantly. "So what if he did? He couldn't help it. His mum was bad again. He said he couldn't bear not to stay with her when she's sick. It just goes to show what a really nice boy he is."

"But Georgia, I think he was lying. I heard him say that he was—" But Aeysha never got to finish the sentence. Georgia turned on her in fury, her eyes blazing in a face that had taken on the pallor of a wax candle.

"I thought you were my friend, Aeysha! But you're not. You're just a nasty little gossip. Alex and I were right to keep things secret, away from the prying eyes and ears of people like you. Go away, I don't want to talk to you."

Aeysha's heart felt as if someone had skewered it, as if something had been broken that would never fully mend. "OK, Georgia, I'll back off," she said, quietly. "But remember I'll always be here if you need me."

"I won't need you," snapped back Georgia.

Aeysha walked to the door, heavy-hearted. Outside she burst into tears and leaned her forehead against the cool wall. Everything had been horrible since Alex arrived at the school. She'd worried that he would tear Georgia and Olivia's friendship apart, but she'd never imagined that he would come between her and her best friend.

Everything seemed so bleak. She tried to comfort herself by thinking about the final of the songwriting contest, but without Georgia there to support her, it just wouldn't be the same. She was missing her already.

Chapter Twenty-Six

Georgia and Alex were sitting together on the windowsill of the rehearsal room that overlooked the path down to the river. Alex was listening to Georgia with his eyes narrowed.

"So she says she overheard me on the bus?" he asked. Georgia nodded. "Well, well, well, who'd have thought that little Aeysha was cut out for a career in the secret service," said Alex, and there was a sneer in his voice that made Georgia feel uncomfortable.

Alex grinned. "It's obvious, isn't it? She's just jealous and she thinks I'm going to take you away from her and the others."

"That's what I thought," said Georgia, eagerly. "But she'll just have to deal with it. I'd much rather spend time with you, anyway, instead of Aeysha and the others. I've grown out of being with them."

An anxious look flashed across Alex's face. "Don't say that. They're your friends. I don't want to keep you from them even if they haven't exactly welcomed me into their little group with open arms. You shouldn't stop going about with them. Besides, I like to hear what you get up to together and what's happening down at the river with Jack. You know he's one of my heroes."

"They're all off to see him in a minute," said Georgia.

"Well, you'd better hurry then, or they'll go without you," said Alex quite sharply.

Georgia looked at him, surprised. "But I'm not going to go, not after what Aeysha said to me. There's sure to be an atmosphere. It would be really awkward. Anyway, I want to hang out with you."

"Actually, I've got things to do," said Alex. "Run along and you can ring me later and tell me everything."

Georgia felt hurt, but Alex had already scrambled off the windowsill and was holding open the door. "Quick, Georgia, you don't want to miss them."

Georgia felt as if he was trying to get rid of her and she wasn't entirely sure she liked his tone. She was torn between standing her ground and wanting to please him. In the end, the latter feeling won out, but she felt she had compromised herself in some way.

"I'll call you later," she said.

"I can't wait," said Alex, turning the full force of his smile upon her. "Every minute will feel like an hour."

Georgia looked at him. "Alex," she said, slowly, "where *were* you last night?"

"I told you, I was safe at home looking after my poor old mum. My dad, he had to go to a business meeting. He may be in with a shot of a US tour. My mum was bad and couldn't be left alone." He considered Georgia's wan face. "Trust me, babe. I'd never lie to you."

Georgia beamed. "I know that."

Alex watched her go, a tiny hint of sadness in his eyes. Georgia was so trusting she made him want to protect her from himself.

"Do you think it's true?" asked Olivia.

The Swans and Pablo were gathered in the

little tent that provided Jack with some shelter when he came off the wire.

Pablo shrugged. "It could be that they're putting out false information to make us over-confident. But from what I hear it seems to be true. Viktor is in pretty bad shape. He's spent the last couple of days mostly in his hammock. When he's been out on the wire, he seems to have difficulty staying on it. He's showing all the signs of mental and physical exhaustion. And if he really is suffering from exhaustion, he'll have to throw in the towel. The conditions are just too awful."

Olivia's phone began to ring. Kasha. She let it go to voicemail, too distracted to talk to him now.

"So you'd be the winner, Dad," said Eel.

Jack shook his head. "I'd still have to get through the last ten days, but I reckon if Viktor was gone all the pressure would be off and it would be a cinch. It's the competition that creates the stress."

"But," said Olivia, "it works the other way too. Even if Viktor is at his lowest ebb, he'd get a tremendous boost if you were out of the running."

"Yes," said Pablo, "that's why we've got to be extra vigilant and make sure Jack keeps his strength up over the next few days." He turned to Jack. "Time you got back on. When are you planning your next break?"

"About one in the morning," said Jack.

"OK," said Pablo. "It's such a wild night I'm going to send most of the security team off to get some sleep. That still leaves me and one other guy to keep watch tonight, and there'll be people nearby if we need reinforcements. With this foul weather, though, I reckon we won't have any trouble."

They all said their goodbyes and started the walk back to the Swan.

"Aeysha," said Olivia, suddenly. "Is everything all right between you and Georgia?" She looked ahead to where Georgia and Tom were walking together.

Aeysha gave a wan little smile. "I thought you were supposed to be the unobservant one, Livy."

"It's just things seem really tense between you."

Aeysha sighed. "We've had a disagreement. We're not talking."

Olivia's eyes were wide. "Not talking? It must be pretty serious."

"She thinks I'm trying to interfere in her life."

"It wouldn't have anything to do with Alex Parks, would it?" asked Olivia.

Aeysha shrugged her shoulders. "I'd love to tell you, Livy, but I can't say. She'll feel completely betrayed if she finds out I've been talking about her. I don't want her to think worse of me than she already does."

Olivia suddenly remembered her missed phone call. "Did you tell Kasha about the songwriting final?"

"I left him a message," said Aeysha, "but he hasn't called me back. I expect he's really busy. He's got his first gig coming up soon."

Chapter Twenty-Seven

Viktor staggered off the wire and half-fell into the arms of one of his team.

"I can't go on," he murmured.

"Get him in the tent," said Ethan, brusquely. "We don't want anyone spotting him in this state. I've got the doctor waiting."

"The doctor?" There was a glimmer of hope in Viktor's eyes. "He will certify I can't go on. He must. Then I'll be able to get some sleep."

"In your dreams," snorted Ethan, unsympathetically. "He'll give you a shot to keep you going."

"I can't, Ethan. I can't go back out there."

Ethan put his face very close to Viktor's pale one. "You can and you will," he said. "I've too much riding on this to let Jack Marvell carry off the prize now. I promise you, Viktor, if you can just hang on for another couple of days Jack Marvell will be gone and the way will be clear."

"How can you be certain?" asked Viktor, exhaustedly. "He's got guts. He won't give up easily."

"Oh, I don't think he'll have any choice," said Ethan, with a grim little chuckle. "I'm going to make quite sure of that."

Viktor looked horrified. "I didn't sign up for this," he whispered. "You promised me there'd be no dirty tricks."

"I didn't realise at the time that you had so much growing up to do," said Ethan crushingly. "You don't really have a choice, Viktor. Walk away now and you will forever be known as Viktor the loser."

Viktor looked as if he was about to weep.

"Come along, boy," said Ethan. "Let's give you that shot. You know that I've got your best interests at heart. I've invested a lot in you."

Viktor didn't have the strength to argue. He just wanted to lie down and sleep for a week.

It was turning into another wild night down at the river. The snow was coming down in great squally blasts and the wire was becoming treacherous. Jack almost slipped twice as he walked gingerly towards the river's edge. He shivered. His thoughts were as dark as the night. There were still another ten days before he'd sleep in a warm comfortable bed again.

The nights were always the longest. Sometimes, when he was lying in his flimsy hammock being buffeted by the wind and feeling the damp seep into his bones, he fantasised about soft, warm duvets, fluffy eiderdowns and clean white pillows. He felt as if he hadn't slept for a year. Everything he did required an almost super-human effort. For the first time in his life, he doubted his own strength and ability to succeed in the task he had set himself.

He unclipped his safety wire and stepped on to firm ground. "The wire's slippery," he said to Pablo, gruffly.

"I'll deal with it," said Pablo. He helped Jack into the small shelter. There was just one other member of the team there, at the ready with hot food and drinks and warm, dry clothes. It would just be the two of them on duty that night, taking turns to check that nobody went near the wire.

Pablo stuck his head out of the tent. The snow had turned to sleet, the extra-wet kind that always finds a way to get down the back of your neck. He slipped on Jack's heavy duty cagoule, with its distinctive *JM* on the back, clipped on the safety harness and started to wipe off the build up of grease that could make the wire so treacherous. He was concentrating so hard that he didn't notice the figure on the bridge filming him.

The alarm bell buzzed to warn Jack that he had just ninety seconds to get back on the wire or he would be in breach of the rules. It was so snug in the little tent. He stood up rather reluctantly and Pablo appeared at the flap of the tent and passed him back his distinctive cagoule. Jack put it on and trudged back down to the river. He had a long night ahead of him. He stepped back on to the wire at exactly 1.10am.

In the small shelter, Pablo rolled out his sleeping bag. "I'm going to get my head down for a few hours, Dave. Wake me at 5am and I'll take over the watch. And wake me if Jack makes contact."

The other man nodded. He went outside and sat under a canopy they had rigged up to keep off the worst of the rain. It was freezing. He felt as if his toes had turned to ice. He watched Jack descend safely into his hammock then glanced back at the little tent. He could hear Pablo snoring. Dave put on his headphones to listen to some music. It would help to keep him alert and awake. And that was why he didn't hear someone coming up behind him or feel the handkerchief soaked in chloroform being pressed over his mouth and nose until it was too late.

A few minutes later, a man wearing a coat with *JM* on the back could be seen stepping off the wire and quietly making his way up towards the shoreline, looking about shiftily as if worried he might be spotted. He headed swiftly into the maze of narrow streets around the bridge and into the shadows. Once there, another man handed him a new jacket and a cap. The man put them on and walked swiftly away.

Pablo woke with a jerk at 4.50am. He was alone. Through the tent flap he could see Dave sitting out front, watching the wire. He hoped the guy had stayed awake for the last four hours. There had been some lapses in the past few nights.

He pulled on some extra layers and went outside. Dave murmured that all was well and then headed off home. The rest of the team would be back at six. Pablo settled down in the shelter with a black coffee. He knew that it was the dark hours before first light that Jack found most difficult and he often came off the wire shortly after 5am for a break. Pablo watched as the first rosy tints of morning began to streak the sky. The time ticked by. Pablo smiled to himself. Maybe Jack was actually having a rare good night's sleep.

Chapter Twenty-Eight

Olivia and Tom walked into the classroom together.

"Oh," said Olivia, "I've forgotten to call Kasha back again. He left a message saying he wanted to talk to me..." She tailed off. There was something very strange about the atmosphere in the classroom. Most people were gathered around one of the computers in the corner of the room. When Kylie saw Olivia, she nudged Connor. People fell silent and turned round to stare.

"What is it?" asked Olivia, urgently.

"I think you'd better see this, Livy," said Kylie. "We thought you must already know about it." She shrugged and looked worried. "But it seems we were wrong."

"Jack...?" asked Olivia, with a quiver in her voice.

The other children parted like a sea to let her see the screen.

Cheat! screamed the headline to the news story, which said that, last night, Jack Marvell had been spotted leaving the wire and checking into a hotel near Tower Bridge. One of the receptionists had filmed him on her phone. Underneath there was a link to an interview with her.

"I recognised him at once," said Tilda Soames. "We have lots of well-known people staying here. We've even had that lovely Kasha Kasparian. So I knew who the man was as soon as he walked in. I've always been a bit of a fan of Jack Marvell. But not any more! He checked in under another name and the room was already booked and paid for. But he seemed so shifty that I filmed him as he headed for the lift. I was so disgusted that somebody of his reputation should be cheating in this way. I knew it was my duty to contact the newspapers."

The video she'd made had been posted below. Olivia clicked on it and gasped.

It wasn't the greatest quality and the man

had a cap pulled down low over his head, but it certainly looked very much like Jack. He moved very much like Jack did and had all the same mannerisms.

Olivia knew it must be a forgery, but she couldn't bear for people to think that her dad was a cheat.

She stood up, knocking over her chair, and ran from the room and out of the Swan towards the river, closely followed by Tom.

"It just gets worse and worse," said Pablo, gloomily. They had retreated to the tent to get away from the photographers and TV crews that were everywhere. "Somebody else has come forward with more video evidence that Jack wasn't on the wire last night." He touched his phone and the video began. This time, Jack had been filmed in Tooley Street, asking directions to the hotel. Olivia's heart was racing. Again the film was pretty blurry, but it certainly looked and sounded a lot like Jack.

"It must be a fake," she said.

Pablo sighed. "Of course, but the people putting this stuff out are convinced it's not. Apparently, they've grilled the receptionist and the night porter backs her up. He thinks it was Jack, too." He paused. "And there's worse. There's a film showing me on the wire wearing Jack's jacket shortly before he checked in. The implication is that I was impersonating him while he slipped away to a hotel for the night. There's even another bit showing him coming off the wire at 1.42am."

"So why were you on the wire last night?" asked Tom.

"I was cleaning off the grease," explained Pablo. "It's got to be done regularly for safety reasons. There was nothing odd about it, except that unfortunately I'd borrowed Jack's jacket when I did it. I didn't know someone was secretly filming me."

"But you must be able to swear that Jack went back on the wire at 1.10am and didn't come off the wire again until 7.12 am?"

Pablo looked worried again. "That's the problem. I can't swear that, and neither can anyone else. I certainly saw him step on to the wire at 1.10am and I saw him come off at first light. I can also swear that he didn't come or go between 5.02am and 7.12am because I was watching the wire. Plenty of other people were

176

with me from six o'clock, too."

"But what about between one and five, then?" asked Olivia.

"I was asleep, and the guy on watch has confessed to falling asleep almost as soon as he sat down, and he didn't wake up again until just after four-thirty. It's odd, because he's normally completely reliable. So, anybody could have come and gone on the wire during that time. We don't have a leg to stand on."

"It's such bad luck," said Tom.

"I don't know how much is down to bad luck," said Pablo. "Most nights there are at least three of us here all the time, sometimes more. It was as if somebody knew that there were only going to be two last night. I'm beginning to think that we've got a mole in our midst."

Just then, a woman popped her head round the flap of the tent. "He's coming off, Pabs," she said.

Pablo stood up with a sigh. "This isn't going to be pretty." He turned to Olivia and Tom. "I think you two'd better go. You are not going to want to see this."

But Olivia refused to leave so they went and stood by the end of the wire. Jack moved along it like a man walking towards his own execution. On the bridge there was a loud crowd of people shouting, "Cheat! Cheat!" As he reached the end of the wire there came the sound of hundreds of camera shutters clicking.

"Are you going to make a statement, Jack?" called the reporters. But Jack said nothing. His face was grey and his eyes looked dull. As he tried to walk towards the tent he was jostled and pulled about by the press, which wasted precious seconds of his break.

"Are you going to give up?" cried one.

"What do you feel about the loss of your reputation?"

"Are you a cheat, Jack Marvell?"

Olivia couldn't bear it. "He's not a cheat," she shouted. "He's the most trustworthy person in the whole world. And I'm going to prove it."

Pablo pushed them into the tent and closed the flap. Olivia threw herself at Jack's neck. He gave her a small, sad smile.

"I hope you *can* prove it, Liv. Because otherwise I'm finished."

When Olivia and Tom got back to the Swan, Alicia, Aeysha, Georgia and Eel were waiting for them in the hall. Eel ran towards her sister and hugged her.

"We saw you on the TV, Livy! You were amazing."

"You were," said Alicia and she looked quite tearful. "We were all enormously proud of you."

"We all totally believe in Jack," said Aeysha, quietly. "We know he's no cheat." Olivia smiled gratefully at Aeysha as she continued, "We're going to do whatever we can to help you prove that he's been set up. We've got to find who's responsible."

"We do," said Olivia. She just wished she knew where to start.

The bell rang and the hall filled with Swans scurrying to their next lesson. When they saw Olivia and the others standing in the hall, they all went quiet. Some averted their eyes and looked embarrassed, a few muttered "Sorry" as they passed by. None of them had seen Olivia's outburst on the TV yet.

"Come," said Alicia, "let's go up to my office and have hot chocolate and talk." Once again the sea of children parted to let Olivia, Alicia and the others make their way up the stairs. As they neared the top, they passed Alex Parks. He was very pale.

"Livy, I'm very sorry about your dad," he said, in a whisper so quiet she could barely hear him.

Chapter Twenty-Nine

Olivia clapped mechanically as the two children on stage finished singing to huge cheers from the back of the Cavendish Hall, where their families were sitting. She'd barely registered the song. She'd been too busy turning over what had happened to Jack in her mind and trying to see if there was something she'd missed. Aeysha had said she wouldn't mind if Olivia hadn't felt like coming to the song contest finals, but Olivia had promised to support her friend and she wasn't going to go back on her word now, especially as Tom hadn't been able to make it either.

The children who had just finished singing were propelled towards the front of the stage by the show's host to face the judges, who were sitting at the front of the auditorium behind a long table. One of the judges started talking about the song and what had impressed her and the things that the songwriters might do to make it even better. Another talked earnestly about key changes and technical stuff that was a complete mystery to Olivia.

She looked at the clock on her phone. It was lucky that Aeysha was the second contestant of the sixteen finalists, or Olivia would be late for the *Dream* rehearsal at Campion's. She had had to stuff her costume into her rucksack together with the high-wire that Sebastian Shaw had asked her to bring along for an idea he wanted to try out. She'd positioned herself at the end of a row near an exit so that after Aeysha had sung her song, and the judges had said their piece, she would be able to slip quietly away.

Aeysha appeared on stage and sat down on a chair with her guitar. Olivia could tell that she was really nervous because she always flicked her hair when she was anxious. The judges gave the signal and Aeysha began playing.

Olivia recognised the song immediately. It was the one she had heard Aeysha playing to Kasha. She'd obviously been working on it further because it was different, more subtle and layered. It was interesting, thought Olivia, the way Aeysha had taken one thing and by just changing a few notes had transformed it into something else.

She guessed that's what art was, a constant borrowing and changing. She'd read enough Shakespeare to know that he seldom made up his own plots, but borrowed them from other writers. Some might call it stealing, but Olivia knew that it was taking inspiration. She listened to the end of the song and smiled. In this instance it was as if Aeysha had stolen from herself, taking what she had originally written and making it into something new and better.

The applause was very loud and very appreciative. It wasn't just Aeysha's family who were making a racket. Everybody in the hall was aware they had heard something special. Olivia clapped as hard as she could, delighted that her friend had set the bar so high for all the other contestants. Olivia didn't know much about music but she felt certain that Aeysha's song would be the one that everyone else would have to beat.

Aeysha moved to the front of the stage, ready to receive the judges' comments. The first one said how refreshing it was to hear a song that was genuinely original, and that he'd never expected to hear a song of that calibre in the competition. He thought that, if she wanted it, Aeysha had a promising future ahead of her as a songwriter.

As he was speaking, Olivia could see one of the other judges bobbing up and down at the end of the table as if she were agitated about something. *Lucie Groves* was the name written on the place card in front of her. The next judge started to give her comments. "I agree with everything that has been said," she said. "This is a truly original piece of work…"

"Actually," interrupted Lucie Groves, standing up. "I must intervene. I can't listen to this any more. I *know* this song. Well, something very like it. I don't think this song is original at all."

Aeysha had gone a deep red colour. "I'm not sure what you're suggesting, Lucie," said the head of the judges. "Do you mean that this child is pretending to have written this song?"

Lucie Groves looked embarrassed. "Maybe

we should discuss this in private," she said, glancing at an increasingly tearful Aeysha.

But at the moment, Aeysha chose to speak. "You think I've copied it from someone!" she cried, desperately. "But I wrote it, I promise I did."

The whole hall was buzzing and the judges were all talking to each other. "It's my song," said Aeysha. "I would never steal somebody else's work."

Aeysha's mother rushed up on to the stage and glared at the panel like a lioness protecting one of her cubs. She held the sobbing Aeysha in her arms. "My daughter is not a cheat," she said, with quiet dignity.

"I'm making no accusations," said Lucie Groves. "But I know this song, or something very like it. That very distinctive part in the chorus, the bit that makes it so original."

"How do you know for certain?" asked one of the other judges.

"Because I am Kasha Kasparian's record producer," said Lucie Groves, "and something very similar is on his as yet unreleased album, which nobody except me and a very few people have even heard yet."

Olivia gasped, and thought back to the day when she had heard Aeysha play Kasha the song at the Swan. She knew what she had heard and she knew for certain that the song was Aeysha's, or at least ninety per cent Aeysha's. It wasn't Aeysha who had stolen the song from Kasha but the other way round.

She suddenly remembered the missed calls from Kasha and how she'd thought there was something odd about his voice saying he wanted to talk to her.

The judges were conferring. They turned to the audience. "We're going to take a short break to try and sort this out. Please bear with us."

They walked up the short flight of steps on to the stage and ushered Aeysha and her mother towards the wings. Aeysha kept repeating tearfully: "I didn't steal it. I'd never do anything like that."

"Wait!" cried Olivia. The judges on the stage turned back towards her expectantly. "I know that Aeysha didn't steal the song. I've heard her sing it before. I heard her sing it to—"

Olivia was about to say Kasha's name but Aeysha interrupted her. "No, Livy. You can't have heard it before."

Everyone looked at her.

"That's pretty much an admission of guilt," said Lucie Groves, with an unexpected gentleness in her voice. "I don't know how you got hold of the song but…" She suddenly hit her forehead. "Of course! Kasha said that he was doing some songwriting workshops, it must have been when he was writing his song." She looked at Aeysha. "Did you go to those? That must be where you heard it and copied it."

"These things do happen," said one of the judges kindly. "You hear something, store it in your subconscious and then you write pretty much the same thing without realising what you are doing. Maybe that's what happened, dear?"

"No!" cried Olivia. But everyone ignored her.

"Perhaps," said one of the other judges, "we could get a copy of Kasha Kasparian's song and compare the two."

"Or you could just ask Kasha," said Olivia, hotly. "Aeysha isn't lying. It is her song. I know it is."

The judges ignored her again and ushered Aeysha and her mum away. As they left the stage Olivia heard Lucie say: "I have to protect my…"

The hall was in uproar. Olivia went over to the rest of Aeysha's family who were shaking their heads in disbelief. "Our Aeysha would never steal anything," said her dad, looking close to tears himself.

"I know that," said Olivia, "and you know that. We're just going to have to make the judges believe it, too."

Chapter Thirty

Georgia and Alex were on the top of the bus together on their way to Campion's for a rehearsal of *A Midsummer Night's Dream*. They had just been to the zoo in Regent's Park and had had a brilliant time. Alex had impersonated the chimpanzees, and he had listened attentively to everything that Georgia had said. They had eaten ice creams and, when Georgia had suggested that they go to the reptile house, Alex had confessed that he was scared of snakes. He had taken Georgia's ribbing with enormous good humour. It was odd, thought Georgia, there was something different about him. Something softer and less confident. The bus stopped to allow people to get off.

"Georgia," said Alex, and his voice was so

tentative that Georgia's heart lurched. She looked at him warily. Something about his serious expression made her think he was about to say something important, maybe something she didn't want to hear. She smiled encouragingly, but her heart was thudding. Was he going to say that he wanted to break up?

"I just wanted to say that I had a really brilliant time today, Georgia," he said.

"Me, too," said Georgia.

"I really like being with you."

Georgia felt her stomach fizz. "I like being with you, too, Alex," she said.

Then, suddenly, his expression changed. "If only you knew, Georgie. I'm not a nice person. I've done some pretty awful things."

Georgia looked at him anxiously. Her encounter with Aeysha flashed across her mind. Had he lied to her?

"What do you mean?" she asked, but then she heard Connor's voice behind them.

"Hello, Georgie," he said, and then rather more coolly: "Hi Alex."

The moment was lost. Alex felt for her hand on the seat between them and squeezed it hard. But his face was full of regret.

* * *

Olivia climbed through the little window of the toilet. She'd tried to get backstage through the stage door but had been turned away. She knew she had to talk to Aeysha.

She'd already tried ringing and texting Kasha several times, but there had been no reply. She had left him a series of increasingly curt messages, telling him what was going on. Olivia scrambled off the windowsill and cautiously opened the door of the bathroom. She quickly closed it again as she saw the judges come out of a dressing room and start to walk down the corridor towards the stage. She waited until they had disappeared into the wings and then she slipped down the corridor and into the room she had just seen them leave.

Aeysha was sitting in front of the make-up mirror weeping and being comforted by her mum. Olivia walked swiftly over to her friend and hugged her tight. Mrs Aziz smiled at her and said that as Livy was there, she would go back to the auditorium to check on her husband and the rest of the family.

"I don't understand why you don't tell them the truth," said Olivia to Aeysha. "Tell them that it's your song. I know it is. I'm a witness to that. I was outside the room that day. I heard you play a version of your song to Kasha. I also know that Kasha was blocked. He had to write one last song for his album and he couldn't do it. So that's why he must've stolen your song out of desperation. You must tell them."

Aeysha raised her head. "I can't do that, Livy. Don't you see? It would completely destroy Kasha's reputation. He's got everything to lose. If it came out that he had taken the song, his career would be over. I can't do that to him. I couldn't live with myself."

"But Aeysha, what about *you*? I won't let you do this. It's insane. Everyone would think that you were a thief, and how would that make your mum and dad feel? It's too awful to contemplate."

Aeysha just shook her head sadly. "I know. But I just can't do it, Livy."

Olivia tried to get Kasha again. No answer. "I wish I knew where he is so we could at least talk to him."

"Haven't you seen the pictures in the paper of all the screaming girls outside the de Wilde hotel? He's holed up there before his tour starts next week."

"Oh really?" said Olivia. "Right, then, I'm going to get him."

"No, Livy," said Aeysha. "Don't do this."

But Olivia was already out of the room. Aeysha put her head down on the dressing-room table. She knew that Olivia was on a wild-goose chase. She'd never get anywhere near Kasha.

Olivia pressed the button on her phone again. And once again, the call went straight to voicemail.

"It's Kasha, I'm busy. Leave a message!" said Kasha's voice.

She sighed loudly and checked the time. She would have to miss the *Dream* rehearsal but this was more important. She guessed everyone would think she'd blown it out because of what was happening to Jack.

She ran all the way to the tube, got on and then got off two stops later. She ran all the way up the escalator and passed through the ticket barriers into the street. She looked at the map on her phone and set off at a jog.

She heard the noise long before she

reached the hotel. Crash barriers had been set up all around the entrance and hundreds of girls were leaning over then excitedly. Some of them were screaming, which Olivia thought was particularly silly as there was no sign of anything or anyone to scream at.

Every now and again a girl would make a rush for the entrance of the hotel only to be pushed back again gently by one of the many security guards who were gathered around the door. Olivia watched the scene, quite astonished by the passion of the girls, several of whom were holding up large pictures of Kasha.

She tried his number again, but there was still no answer. There was nothing for it, she would just have to blag her way into the hotel. She took a deep breath and started walking towards the entrance. A path had been cleared between two crash barriers that had been set up to keep Kasha's fans at bay. She tried to look as confident as possible, but inside she felt like a wobbly jelly. Several of the girls behind the crash barriers watched her with undisguised interest. But she hadn't got very far when two burly security guards stepped in front of her.

"Can we help you, miss?" asked one.

Olivia thought quickly. "My aunt," she said. "She's staying here."

The men considered her. "And what would your aunt's name be, miss?" asked one, producing a clipboard with a long list of names. He was obviously going to check that she was telling the truth.

Olivia hesitated just a fraction too long. "Brown," she said. "Her name is Belinda Brown."

The man looked down the list. He smiled kindly at her. "Nice try, love, but we're not going to fall for that one."

"Listen," said Olivia urgently, "I've got to get into the hotel. I've got to see someone. It's a matter of life and death."

The men looked at each other and raised their eyebrows. "Would this someone be called Kasha Kasparian, by any chance?" said the taller of the two, looking amused.

"Look," said Olivia. "I'm from the school Kasha went to before he was famous. I know him. He's a friend. He'll want to see me. I know he will."

The shorter of the two men laughed and

waved an arm at all the shrieking girls. "They all say that. They're all Kasha Kasparian's best friend."

"But this is different. I really do know him. Look!" She got out her phone and scrolled down her contacts. She jabbed her finger at Kasha's name. "Look! It's his number."

The men shook their heads. "In your dreams, love," said the tall one.

Olivia knew it was no good. She would never talk her way past these men. Suddenly she made a break for the hotel entrance, hoping desperately that if she could only just get inside she would be able to find her way to Kasha's room. She nimbly side-stepped a security guard who was coming towards her with his arms outstretched. Applause went up from the crowd. It spurred her on and she had almost made it to the revolving door when she was grabbed, lifted off her feet and passed over the crash barrier into the crowd of girls.

She felt tears tickle at the back of her eyes. She knew she was being silly, and even if she *had* made it inside the hotel, she didn't have a clue where she would find Kasha. She wasn't just going to bump into him. She might just as well give up and go to rehearsal. She couldn't help Aeysha clear her name any more than she could help her dad. She was a complete failure.

The two girls she was standing by eyed her sympathetically. "That was amazing, you almost made it," said one of them.

Olivia sniffed, and the other girl handed her a clean tissue.

"I'm Imy, and this is Gem."

"We understand just how you feel," said Gem, "it's so hard being so close to him but so far, too. I know that if he realised how much we cared, he'd come and see us. He'd realise that we're his real fans, that we're not like all the others, that we really love him."

Olivia looked at Imy and Gem's fresh, shining faces. When she had arrived outside the hotel and seen the girls, she had dismissed them as idiots and obsessives. But there was something about their fervor that was touching.

It made her think of Georgia when she had been pining after Alex. And at least Alex had been real; these girls were hankering after something unattainable. The closest they might ever come to Kasha was a scrawled autograph or a touch of the fingertips.

She wondered if Kasha had any inkling how much he meant to them, how big he loomed in their lives, how grateful he ought to be for the passion and love that they poured into him because without them he would be nothing.

"How long have you been waiting outside the hotel?" she asked curiously.

"Since Friday after school," said Imy and Gem together proudly.

They saw Olivia's surprised face. "Oh," said Gem simply. "You do anything for love. Real love. Kasha is worth it."

"Do you sleep here?" asked Olivia astonished.

Imy and Gem shook their heads. "We'd like to, but our parents won't let us. Imy's dad is the building manager in the office block at the back of the hotel. He drops us off in the morning and picks us up when he leaves in the evening."

Imy looked at Gem. "Shall we show her?" Gem nodded and Imy opened her mobile phone and showed Olivia a photo.

At first Olivia couldn't work out what it was, but then she realised that it was the back of the hotel. The photo showed one particular balcony, high up on the fifth floor.

"That's it," said Imy, dreamily. "That's his room."

"How do you know?" asked Olivia.

"Yesterday, my dad let us come up to his office, and while we were there Kasha briefly appeared on the balcony. He looked so sad. We weren't quick enough to get a pic of him, but now we know which room he's in. We're the only ones who do."

"But if all you want is a glimpse of him, and his room's round the back, what are you doing waiting out the front?" asked Olivia.

"He's got to come out this way at some point," answered Gem. "The road round the back is blocked off. We can't get close round the back, anyway. The place is crawling with security guards checking anyone who goes in or comes out of the building. If you try to go anywhere near the back, they just shoo you this way."

Olivia suddenly had a mental image of young girls being herded like sheep by shaggy sheepdog security guards.

"We're the lucky ones," sighed Imy. "We've seen the actual room he's in. Where he sleeps, and everything. I wanted Dad to let us stay in his office all day, but he said he'd get the sack if his boss caught us there."

"If we'd stayed in that storeroom, though, nobody would ever have known we were there," said Gem. "We could've watched in case he came out on to the balcony again."

"What storeroom?" asked Olivia, quickly.

"There's a storeroom with a little window that looks almost directly on to Kasha's balcony. If he came out, you'd be just a few metres away. You might even be able to speak to him!" Imy's eyes were shining.

"Imy," said Olivia urgently, "do you think you could get me inside your dad's building and show me the storeroom?"

Imy looked anxious. "Well, I could, 'cos the security guard on the desk downstairs knows me and he'd let me in. But I wouldn't want to get my dad into trouble or anything."

"If we're clever about it," said Olivia, "nobody will ever know we've been there. Please, Imy, this is really important."

"OK," said the girl. "I can tell you're a true fan, like us. That you really love Kasha. But it can only be a quick look, just for a few minutes."

"I'll only need a few minutes," said Olivia,

with a smile. She looked at them. "And if my plan works, I promise that you too will get to meet Kasha Kasparian."

Imy and Gem's faces lit up with pure joy.

"Come on, then!" said Imy.

Chapter Thirty-One

Imy walked confidently up to the reception desk with Gem and Olivia behind her. The security guard sitting there smiled at her.

"Hello, Imy. Do you want to see your dad? I'll see if he's free, shall I?" He went to pick up the phone.

"Actually, he's expecting us," said Imy, quickly. "I've just spoken to him. We need to leave some stuff with him. He said to go straight up to the fifth floor where he's doing some repairs."

The man smiled. "No problem. You know the way, don't you? Out the lift and turn right."

The doors of the lift opened. Imy peered out cautiously to check there was nobody in the corridor and then she pulled the others across the corridor and pushed them through an unmarked door. She closed the door behind them. They were in a narrow room with shelves stacked with files on both walls. At the end of the room was a window facing out on to the back of the hotel.

Olivia moved swiftly towards the window, pushed it open and leaned out. It was on a level with a room with a balcony that had a metal rail running along its top.

"See," breathed Imy. "That's Kasha's room."

"Are you absolutely sure?" asked Olivia. "This is *definitely* the balcony where you saw Kasha?"

"Yes," said Gem indignantly. "We wouldn't get something like that wrong. It's too important. It's definitely the right one. He was standing right there."

"Good," said Olivia. She looked down. There were several security guards milling around below, but they didn't notice her looking at them. It was something Olivia had observed before: very few people ever looked upwards, particularly in London. The real threat would come if anybody looked out the window of the offices and saw her. She just hoped that as it was Saturday nobody would be there, except Imy's dad. She took off her rucksack, opened it and pulled out the wire.

"What's that?" asked Gem, curiously.

"Wait and see," said Olivia. She looked down again to check that the security guards weren't looking, then she threw one end of the wire as hard as she could across the divide between the buildings. It hooked easily on to the rail over the balcony.

She pulled it tight and hooked it under the windowsill of the store room. It wasn't ideal, but it would have to do. Jack would be furious with her if he saw her taking such a risk. But she had no choice, and she was confident it would hold.

"Look, Imy, Gem," she said urgently, putting her rucksack back on. "This is my mobile number and I'll need yours." She reeled it off and Imy entered it in her phone and gave Olivia her number. "In a second I'm going to walk across the wire to Kasha's room. When I get to the other side I'm going to unhook the wire and I want you to pull it back across here, unhook it from the sill and then leave, taking it with you. Go back to where you were at the front of the hotel and I'll meet you there in a short while, probably about fifteen minutes or so. I'll call if there's any problem."

Imy and Gem were staring at her, open-mouthed.

"You're going to walk across that wire to get into Kasha's room?" stuttered Imy.

Olivia nodded. "It's only a little walk. I know how to do it. It won't be hard."

"But if you fall, you'll be killed," said Imy, looking scared.

"Yes, but I won't fall," said Olivia, patiently.

"But to take such a risk, just in the hope of seeing Kasha. You must be his greatest fan ever," said Gem, wonderingly, as Olivia jumped on to the windowsill.

"Well, I just hope he realises how lucky he is," said Olivia, tartly. She stepped out on to the wire. Biggest fan? What she'd like to do most at this particular moment was wring Kasha Kasparian's neck.

Chapter Thirty-Two

Olivia stepped over the rail and on to Kasha's balcony. She looked down. As she'd guessed, the security guards below were completely oblivious to the fact that she had just walked straight above their heads on to the balcony of the person they were supposed to be protecting.

She didn't know how she was going to get into his room. If the balcony door was locked, she was just going to have to knock. Carefully she put her hand on the door handle and pushed it down. It gave easily. She turned back to Imy and Gem, gave them the thumbs up, and unhooked the wire so the girls could haul it back to the store room.

"Good luck," mouthed Imy.

Olivia gave them a wave, turned and,

as quietly as she could, entered the room. She realised at once that she was not in a hotel bedroom but in the living room of a suite. She had been in one before at the Savoy where the Hollywood twins, Cosmo and Cosima Wood, had been staying while they were in London. That had been very grand with a dining room, a vast living area, a kitchen and three bedrooms. It was like an apartment within a hotel.

This was smaller but very swish. There were two closed doors leading off the living room, and Olivia guessed that one was a bathroom and the other was a bedroom. She glanced around. From the state of the room, she knew that this was definitely where Kasha was staying. The place was a tip. Several pairs of jeans, half-drunk cans of Coke and discarded magazines were littered all over the floor. Kasha's beloved, battered old guitar stood in the corner, and there was a stack of photos of him on a small table, ready for signing.

So where was he? She suddenly realised how awful it would be if someone came into the room and found her there. They would probably think she was a stalker and have her arrested. For a moment she wished that she hadn't asked

Imy and Gem to remove the wire. Now she had no escape route.

Maybe Kasha had gone out? Maybe he was somewhere else in the hotel? She moved towards one of the doors and as she did so, she heard a sound. It was such an odd sound. It sounded like a small animal, maybe a rabbit or a hamster in pain. Slowly and carefully she pushed the door open. The curtains were drawn and the room was in darkness, but she could make out the bed with its rumpled covers. She took a step further into the room, peered into the gloom and realised that Kasha was curled up in a ball on the bed, a picture of abject misery.

He suddenly realised she was there. For a moment, they just looked at each other in shock, and then he said: "Have you come to kill me, Livy? It would be the kindest thing to do. Just put me out of my misery."

Olivia could tell from the hopeless tone of his voice that he wasn't entirely joking. But she was irritated nonetheless. "Don't be so dramatic, Kasha. Besides, killing is way too good for you. Do you know what you've done? You've made the sweetest, nicest, kindest girl in the world look like a thief and a cheat."

Kasha looked up at her, his beautiful eyes dark with despair. "I know exactly what I've done, Livy. As soon as I got your messages, I knew."

"Well, stop whimpering, then, and put it right."

"But I don't know how to!" said Kasha.

"I'm going to help you sort things out," said Olivia. "And *then* I'm going to kill you, Kasha Kasparian."

Chapter Thirty-Three

Kasha had been to the bathroom, washed his face, and was looking far more presentable. Olivia had thrust two of his photos at him as soon as he appeared and ordered him to sign them.

"I don't think this is the time for autographs," complained Kasha.

"I owe someone," said Olivia, "and, unlike some people, I always acknowledge my debts."

Chastened, Kasha did what she asked without a murmur.

"Right," said Olivia, brusquely, as soon as he was finished. "Let's get out of here. We've got to hurry, or we'll be too late. The contest will be over and Aeysha will have lost her chance and her reputation will be in tatters."

Kasha stared at her. "But, Livy, I can't just walk out of here! If I try to leave by the front, I'll be crushed by all the girls out there, and there's loads of security at the back of the building. They wouldn't let me leave."

Olivia frowned. "You mean, you're some kind of prisoner?"

"No, not exactly," said Kasha, "but with the first concert next week the record company and the promoters are taking no chances. It's been made quite clear that I'm expected to stay here and not go anywhere except for rehearsals at the venue. I reckon that if I try to leave the hotel with you, I'll be turned back. Ever so politely, of course, but very firmly."

"So this room is really a sort of luxury cell," said Olivia, shaking her head in disbelief.

"I guess that's one way of putting it," said Kasha. "They think of it as protecting their investment. They've put a lot of money into me. They want to make sure they don't lose it. So if I say that I'm just popping out for a bag of crisps, let alone to 'fess up to stealing somebody else's song, I don't think they're going to be keen to let me go. They've sold squillions of pounds worth of tickets for the concerts. I'd be putting all that at risk."

"So how are we going to get you out of here?" asked Olivia. She'd been so taken up with trying to get into the hotel that it had never crossed her mind that Kasha might not just be able to stroll out of it.

'I don't have a clue; ideas are strictly your department," said Kasha. "How did you get in?"

"Over the wire and on to the balcony," said Olivia.

"Ah," said Kasha. "And there was I wondering whether you'd added lock-picking to your increasingly wide range of skills. But the wire definitely isn't an option for me."

"I haven't got it anyway," said Olivia, gloomily. She checked her phone. Time was ticking by. She had a couple of texts from Tom, who was at the *Midsummer Night's Dream* rehearsal and wondering where she was. *Dream!* Suddenly Olivia knew just how to get Kasha out of there. She opened her rucksack and began to pull out the contents.

"I've just had an idea," she said. "It's so brilliant, it may just work."

* * *

212

"Ready, Kasha?" asked Olivia, as the lift descended to the lobby.

"Yes," said Kasha, "but don't go too fast or I'll fall flat on my face. Walking's quite tricky in these high-heeled boots. *And* they're totally killing my feet. And this stupid veil means I can't see where I'm going."

"Here we are," said Olivia, as the lift doors opened. "Whatever you do, try and avoid speaking to anyone, and keep your head down so your face is hidden."

They stepped out into the busy lobby. Kasha stumbled and grabbed Olivia's arm for balance. "Careful," she hissed.

They walked across the wide expanse of the lobby. Olivia felt as if everyone was staring at them, but nobody seemed to be taking any interest at all. They reached the front entrance of the hotel and through the glass doors Olivia could see the waiting girls and the security men. She took a deep breath.

"Here we go," she whispered. She guided Kasha towards the doors but just before they got there, a doorman wearing a top hat and livery stepped towards them. For a terrible moment Olivia thought that he was going to stop them from leaving, but he simply held the door wide open, raised his hat and said: "Have a lovely time, ladies."

Olivia gave him a dazzling smile and replied, "Thank you, we will." She looked firmly ahead as they stepped towards the sea of girls. The girls craned their necks to see who was coming through the door but lost interest as soon as they could see it was just a girl accompanied by an elegant young woman. The woman was dressed in a smart 1930s style suit, button boots and a rather dashing little hat with a veil and a small feather stuck jauntily in it. The hat was tilted at such an angle that it almost totally obscured her face.

Olivia and Kasha started walking down the path between the crash barriers. The security guards merely glanced at them. Olivia held her breath. They had almost reached the end of the path when Olivia saw the pair of security guards who had stopped her entering the hotel looking with interest at them. One of them stood up, and walked steadily towards them. Olivia tried to look nonchalant.

"We may be going to have to run," she hissed out of the side of her mouth.

"Run?" hissed back Kasha. "In these heels?"

The security guard loomed up in front of them, blocking their way. "You're the girl from earlier, aren't you?" he said. "The one who said she had an aunt staying in the hotel?" Olivia nodded. "Is this your aunt?" Olivia nodded vigorously again.

"Well, I don't know how you got into the hotel, but I clearly owe you an apology. I'm sorry I didn't believe your niece, madam."

Something like a squeak came out from under Kasha's hat, and Olivia quickly covered it by saying: "She's got terrible laryngitis. She can't speak. But there's no need to apologise. It was my fault. I forgot Belinda was using her maiden name. But everything's fine now."

The man smiled. "And I don't suppose you got lucky and saw Kasha Kasparian, too, did you?"

Olivia shook her head. "Oh, I'm not all that bothered about him. He's no great shakes."

She felt Kasha tug furiously at her sleeve, and they walked through the crowd and on to the street. In front of them, she saw Imy and Gem, their faces shining with excitement.

"What happened? Did you get into Kasha's room? Did you see him?" they asked, taking absolutely no notice of the woman standing at Olivia's side.

Olivia nodded and felt around in her rucksack. "These are for you," she said, producing the two photographs that she had got Kasha to sign.

Imy and Gem looked at them. "To Imy, all my love, Kasha," whispered Imy.

"And he's done one for me, too," smiled Gem, dreamily.

"He's the kindest, most generous, most amazing boy in the entire world," said Imy.

"Mmm," said Olivia dryly. "I wouldn't go quite that far." She paused. "Listen, you've been really brilliant but my … aunt and I have got to run."

"But we want to hear everything that Kasha said to you and what his room is like and everything," said Gem, her voice full of disappointment.

"Disgustingly untidy," said Olivia. "Listen, I'll tell you more, but not now. I promise. I never forget a favour and you've both done me one today. Call me later. Kasha is going to make sure that you get tickets to his concert and meet him afterwards."

Imy and Gem were squealing so loudly that they didn't hear Kasha yelp: "Is he?"

"Yes," said Olivia, very firmly, "he is. It's the very least he can do after all the trouble he's put everyone to."

Chapter Thirty-Four

The *Dream* rehearsal had gone well, despite Olivia not turning up. Everyone had waited for a short while to see if she would arrive. When she hadn't appeared ten minutes after the start time, Kylie had been drafted in to play Hermia instead.

Tom was worried about Olivia, but he couldn't help losing himself as the play unfolded. He watched Connor's Lysander swear his love for Georgia's Helena:

> *"Why should you think that I should woo in scorn?*
> *Scorn and derision never come in tears:*
> *Look, when I vow, I weep; and vows so born,*
> *In their nativity all truth appears."*

The scene had continued as Alex's Demetrius awoke from Puck's enchantment and, as if seeing Helena for the very first time, cried:

"O Helen! Goddess, nymph, perfect, divine!
To what, my love, shall I compare thine eye?"

Tom had found himself leaning forward as Alex continued the speech. The way he spoke the words and the way he held Georgia in his gaze, seemed far more than acting. It was almost as if he'd been expressing what he really felt.

After the rehearsal, Alex and Georgia met in a café far enough away from Campion's that there was no risk of running into any other Swans. A TV fixed on the wall was tuned to a twenty-four-hour news channel. The station was running a long story about Jack and how he had been exposed as a cheat. The reporter expressed shock at Jack's refusal to admit his guilt and marvelled at his nerve in continuing the stunt.

Ethan Rees from Viktor's team was saying that Jack should do the decent thing: give up and admit that the best man had won. A live camera zoomed in on Jack, crouching miserably on the wire.

"It's so awful," sighed Georgia. "Jack is destroyed and he's such a nice man."

"Let's go," said Alex suddenly. "I can't bear to watch it."

"Me, neither," said Georgia. "I just hope Livy can prove that the films are forged. It's such a scummy thing to do."

Alex looked pained. "Listen, Georgie, I'm sorry, but I've got to go. I need to talk to my dad. He texted me earlier to say he was near here, visiting his half-sister, Matty. But she'll have gone to work by now and I want to catch up with him. I'll call you later."

Olivia gave Kasha's behind a huge shove and he shot through the window of the ladies' at the Cavendish Hall. Olivia clambered in behind him, and handed him his jeans and T-shirt from her rucksack.

"Here," she said shortly, "you change into these while I go and find Aeysha." She just hoped all this effort hadn't been in vain. She ran into the dressing room where she'd left her friend and found Aeysha pacing up and down, nervously.

"Am I in time?" demanded Olivia.

"Depends what you want to be in time for. My execution?" said Aeysha, gloomily. "The last person is singing now. But it's no good, Livy, the courier came with a copy of Kasha's album and the judges listened to it during the interval and they've decided that I'm definitely a cheat. Two of them thought that the songs had similarities but were still quite different from each other, but Lucie Groves was having none of it. They've told me that when the result is announced I'll be disqualified." Aeysha burst into tears. "I feel so ashamed."

Olivia put her arms around her. "You've got nothing to be ashamed of, Aeysha. It's Kasha who stole your song."

"Well, he did and he didn't," said Aeysha. "He certainly borrowed from it, but he didn't steal it. He turned it into something else. He made it his. I've heard it. It is actually rather brilliant." She paused. "Did you find him?"

"Yes," said Olivia, "he's in the ladies' changing out of his dress."

Aeysha goggled. "Dress?"

"Don't ask," said Olivia. "I'll explain later. Come on."

She took Aeysha by the hand and they went out into the corridor, where they found Kasha. When he saw Aeysha, he looked as if he was going to burst into tears.

"Aeysh, I'm so sorry," he said, with a quiver in his voice.

"It's too late to be sorry," said Olivia sharply. "Aeysha's reputation is in tatters. Only you can fix things by going out there and telling the judges the truth."

Kasha swallowed hard. "OK," he said. "I'll do it."

"We'll be with you," said Olivia. "Every step of the way."

Olivia, Aeysha and Kasha stood at the side of the stage hidden behind the curtain. The judges were standing at the front of the stage. They had been giving brief summing up notes on each of the songs.

"And that completes the line-up. We have had to disqualify Aeysha Aziz, because of the similarity her song has to a forthcoming single from Kasha Kasparian," said the judge. "So," he continued, "to the winners—"

"Stop!" Kasha walked on to the stage, followed by Aeysha and Olivia who were holding hands. A buzz went around the hall as people recognised the young pop star.

A look of horror flashed across Lucie Groves' face. "Kasha," she said warningly. "What on earth are you doing here?" She walked over to him and hissed in his ear. "I'd strongly advise you to keep your mouth shut."

"No, I won't keep my mouth shut," said Kasha, loudly. "Aeysha is being accused of being a cheat and she's not. She's a really talented songwriter and the song you heard today is the song she wrote in the songwriting workshop that I ran at the Swan."

"And it's all her own work?" chipped in one of the judges.

Kasha paused. "I just made a few suggestions that she took on board, but for all I know she might have worked on it since."

Aeysha nodded.

"So the question is," asked the judge, "how did something so similar end up on your album?"

Lucie Groves began to look even more worried. She didn't liked the way this was going. She shot another warning look at Kasha.

"I … I was having difficulty writing the last song for the album so I—"

"I gave it to him," chipped in Aeysha, quickly. "I gave it to him to do what he wanted with. It was a gift from me to him."

"So the song belongs to Kasha?" asked the judge. "But it was written by you?"

"Yes," said Aeysha. "Except for the bit he helped me with. That bit we wrote together."

The judge turned to Kasha. "Is what Aeysha is saying correct?"

Kasha shot Aeysha a grateful look. "If Aeysha says so," he said with a grin. "I wouldn't like to contradict her."

"I think we need to confer," said the judge, looking at the others. "Kasha, how old are you?"

"Seventeen," he replied.

The judges went into a little huddle, and then emerged smiling. The audience were completely gripped by the unfolding drama and a ripple of excitement went through the room as the chair of the judges stepped to the front of the stage.

"I'm now going to announce the winners of this year's contest," he said, grandly. "In third place: St Philip's School in Trowbridge for Year Eight's collaboration, 'Halcyon Blues'. In second place: Kate Hardcastle for 'The Rain Song'. And," here the judge paused for maximum effect, "in first place: Aeysha Aziz and Kasha Kasparian for their joint effort, 'Untitled'!"

The audience went crazy, and Olivia jumped up and down with delight. Aeysha and Kasha stared at each other in amazement, before breaking into huge grins and hugging.

The judge seized Aeysha's hand and started pumping it up and down. "Congratulations, my dear," he said. "It is a remarkable piece of work."

"Yes," said Lucie Groves, through gritted teeth. "It is."

"Lucie," said Kasha, casually. "I suppose this means that Aeysha should get a writing credit on 'Bruised'. And royalties."

"A writing credit, yes," snapped Lucie shortly. "Royalties, no. She said she gave you the song." She paused as an idea popped into her head. "But, of course, she would get royalties on any songs you wrote together in the future. The two of you could be quite a partnership."

Kasha grinned. "I'd like that."

Aeysha beamed and they high-fived each

other, before Aeysha turned to Olivia and gave her a big hug. "Thank you, Livy," she whispered. "You're the best."

As they made their way backstage, still buzzing with excitement, Lucie turned to Kasha. "How on earth did you get out of the hotel?" she asked.

"Transformation," said Kasha, winking at Olivia. "It's easy when you know how."

"I'll order a taxi to take you back," said Lucie.

"Actually, no, Lucie," said Kasha. "I want to go home, to my own place. Nobody will know, they'll all think I'm still at the hotel."

"I don't think that's a good idea," said Lucie, quickly. "Goodness knows what more trouble you'll get into. I need to protect my investment..."

"I'm not an investment," said Kasha, quietly. "I'm a human being, and one who has a good idea for a song buzzing around in his head." There was something about the quiet authority in his voice that made Lucie realise Kasha wasn't going to be pushed around any more.

"In that case, I'll order you a taxi home,"

she said, with a bright smile.

"I'll drop you two on the way," said Kasha to Aeysha and Olivia.

"OK. But we need to make a detour. I'm not finished with you yet," said Olivia.

Chapter Thirty-Five

Kasha got out of the taxi. He grinned at the girls. "I won't be long. You wait there."

"You *are* certain you know what she looks like?" said Olivia, anxiously. "You don't want to look at her photo one more time?" She waved her phone at him.

"No, I'm cool," said Kasha. "Tilda Soames' face is etched on my brain. Besides I reckon she'll be wearing a name tag if she's on duty."

Olivia crossed her fingers as Kasha disappeared through the hotel's revolving doors. Aeysha sat back in the taxi, stroking the engraved cup that she and Kasha had been given as Young Songwriters of the Year.

"Do you really think the receptionist is

part of some kind of plot against Jack?" asked Aeysha.

Olivia shrugged. "It's just a hunch. I've looked at the videos again and again, and there's just something about the way she talks that doesn't ring true to me. She's just a little bit too eager."

"But all the journalists would have checked out whether she has any connection with Viktor, wouldn't they? What could Kasha find out that they couldn't?"

"I don't know," said Olivia. "But when she was talking to the journalists she'd have had her guard up. It's just that in the clip she mentioned Kasha, and it's clear she's got a soft spot for him. She might just let slip a crucial piece of information to him, something that will help us. And we sure do need help. Pablo and the team have been doing their best, but so far they haven't come up with anything."

Just then, Kasha appeared and got back into the taxi.

"Talkative lady," he said, with a grin.

"Well, I hope that you can remember every single thing she said," said Olivia. "However tiny." She fished a notebook and pen out of her rucksack and got ready to write.

It was Monday morning and Olivia, Tom, Aeysha and Georgia were all in the computer room before school. Each of them was working at a terminal.

Olivia gave a loud sigh and swung round on her chair. "Nothing. Absolutely nothing that connects Matilda Soames to Viktor Ivanov or Ethan Rees. We're wasting our time. And the bell's going to go soon." She hit her head with the palm of her hand. "We must be missing something!"

"Maybe we need to look at it from another angle?" said Tom. "Instead of trying to prove that it's all some kind of staged set up, maybe we should try and find the mole in the team?"

Olivia looked interested, so Tom continued. "Before the video story broke, we knew that somebody was passing information from Jack's camp to Viktor's. That's how they stole a march over the firework display. So, if we could just find out who it was, maybe that would help us. After all, there's only eight people in the team."

"Let's write down all the names!"

said Georgia excitedly. Olivia started a new document.

"Right," said Tom. "Then we need to add Miss Swan, Eel and all of us. How many does that make?"

"Fifteen," said Georgia, quick as a flash.

Tom leaned over Olivia's shoulder and looked at the list of names. "I'm certain the answer lies in this list. One of those names is the link; if we can find out who it is, we might be a step closer to proving that the videos are faked."

Chapter Thirty-Six

Eel pulled the large, cream envelope that she had snaffled from Mrs Gibbs that morning from under her mattress and held it against her chest. She knew exactly what it was: her destiny. She hugged the envelope tight. She could hardly bear to open it.

It felt as if time had stood still and at this moment she was standing on an invisible line poised exactly between success and failure. Anna Popova and the other teachers at the Imperial had made their decision and that decision was set down in black and white inside the envelope. There was nothing that she or anyone could do to change what was inside the envelope and as soon as she had opened it, all would be revealed to her. But the moment still seemed ripe with possibility as if, at the very moment when her fingers fumbled to tear open the envelope, she existed simultaneously as the child who had got a place at the Imperial and the child who hadn't.

She unfolded the cream paper.

Dear Mr Marvell,

Subject to references and a further appointment with the physiotherapist, we are delighted to be able to offer your daughter, Alicia Marvell, a place at the Imperial next September. We were most impressed with Alicia's potential and as a result we are offering her a full scholarship.

We would be grateful if you would let us know if you will be accepting this place by 3rd March, and please sign and return the enclosed forms.

With best wishes,
Anna Popova.

Underneath was a hand-written line: "Well done, Eel!"

Eel sat back on her haunches. She was in! The Imperial had accepted her! They thought she had what it takes to be a ballerina, or at least she had the potential. So now she knew she wasn't chasing a futile dream. If she had luck on her side, too, maybe she would one day be a prima ballerina.

Eel felt a thrill of excitement swell like liquid gold in her stomach, but underneath it, something else: a pang of loss. If she went to the Imperial she would have to leave the Swan behind her and all she had found there: her grandmother, friendship and a love of dance. She wouldn't be able to spend as much time with Emmy and her family, and she would have to give up tap and jazz, which she really loved, and the chance to try contemporary when she was in the senior school.

She had recently seen a show at The Place Contemporary Dance School with Alicia, and had been intrigued to discover that there were so many different kinds of dance. At the Imperial, her path would be already laid out for her, stretching ahead until the point where she made it into a serious ballet company or she didn't, despite the long years of hard work and dedication to the cause.

She knew that she should be feeling thrilled and was surprised to discover that her feelings were more complex and confusing. She folded up the letter and was putting it thoughtfully back in the envelope when her mobile rang. It was Esme.

"Did you get in?" came her voice.

"Yes," said Eel. "You?"

"Yes," said Esme, but she didn't sound ecstatic. Eel was puzzled. Esme's passion for ballet was obvious. She wouldn't be having the doubts that Eel herself was now experiencing.

"You don't sound too happy."

"Oh, I'm made up," said Esme. "Getting into the Imperial is the best thing in the world. But I won't be able to go."

"Why not?" demanded Eel.

"I didn't get a scholarship," said Esme. "And there's no way we could afford it without one." Esme's voice cracked.

"How many scholarships are there?" asked Eel, in a small voice.

"One," said Esme, gloomily. "At this stage, anyway. I guess I'll have another crack at it when I'm in Year Six."

"Oh, Esme, that's awful. You don't just deserve the scholarship, you really need it."

"Well, I don't know if I deserve it, but I certainly need it," said Esme. "My dad rang the Imperial and spoke to the registrar. She was really nice, and there is a bursary I could get but we'd never find the rest of the money so it's hopeless. The sad thing is, I was so close to getting the scholarship."

"What do you mean?" asked Eel.

"The registrar let slip that it was a really close thing but another girl just squeaked it. I hope that getting it makes as much difference to her as it would have for me. And hey! Who knows, maybe she'll turn it down." She paused. "But whoever heard of anyone turning down a scholarship to the Imperial?"

"Oh, Esme, I'm so, so sorry," said Eel, tearfully.

"Don't get upset, Eel. I'm sorry, banging on like this, I should be congratulating you properly. It's brilliant that you'll be going! I'll think of you there. I just know that you're going to love it."

"Maybe," said Eel in a small voice.

"What's wrong?" asked Esme.

"Oh, I don't know," said Eel. "I think I need to have a good, long think about my future."

Chapter Thirty-Seven

The phone in Alicia's office rang. She picked it up.

"Anna," she said. "How lovely to hear from you! I hope you're well and that everything at the Imperial is good."

"All is very good," replied Anna. "And you, Alicia? Are you fully recovered from your throat infection?"

Alicia frowned. "I'm fit as a fiddle," she said, slightly confused.

"I'm just ringing to offer my congratulations," continued Anna. "You must be thrilled. It is a remarkable achievement that would not have been possible without such fine teaching. It reaffirms my admiration for the Swan."

Alicia was baffled. What *was* Anna talking about? "We try our best," she said, hoping that all would become clear as the conversation unfolded.

"Well," said Anna, "your best is superlative. I wouldn't have thought it possible that a child who has been having ballet lessons for less than eighteen months could possibly win a scholarship to the Imperial. But Eel is a rare talent indeed."

Alicia suddenly felt as if she were in a plummeting lift. "Eel?!" she blurted out, before she could stop herself.

"Oh my goodness!" said Anna. "Maybe the letter has not arrived yet. It was posted first class yesterday, addressed to Eel's father."

Alicia felt dizzy. She tried to collect herself, and said breezily: "Oh, that explains it, then. Jack's still out on the river. It must be sitting in his pile of post."

Alicia was such a consummate actress that Anna didn't notice anything untoward and started chattering on about the audition and how brave Eel had been to come to such a daunting occasion all on her own. Alicia was only half-listening. Her mind was racing. Could

Jack have entered Eel for the Imperial audition without telling her? It was highly unlikely. She thought about Eel's determination to know the full extent of her talent and considered the possibility that Eel had entered herself. She didn't know whether to be aghast or admiring of Eel's drive and self-possession. She had made a fool out of all of them.

At the other end of the phone, Anna was still raving about Eel's gift.

"It's such marvellous news, Anna," said Alicia. "Thank you so much for your thoughtful call. I'll be in touch very, very soon."

Then Alicia sat for a long time, trying to gather her thoughts. Eel would be leaving the Swan! Eventually, she stood up and went downstairs to talk to Mrs Gibbs. As she negotiated the stairs, she felt old, tired and entirely bereft.

"How could you?" demanded Olivia, her eyes blazing. "How could you do such a thing to Gran? She'll be so hurt and upset. After everything she's done for us! For you, and your dancing. Wait till Dad finds out, he's going to be furious!"

Eel shrank away from her sister's fury. "Maybe he doesn't have to know. Maybe Gran doesn't have to know either," said Eel, very quietly.

"What do you mean? You want me to help you deceive them? I won't do it, Eel, it's wrong," yelled Olivia, completely furious.

A few minutes earlier, she had barged into Eel's bedroom without knocking and seen the large envelope addressed to Jack and the letter Eel was reading before her sister had had a chance to hide them. Eel had looked so guilty that Olivia had insisted she explain what she was doing opening Jack's post, and the whole sorry saga had come tumbling out.

"I can't believe that a sister of mine could be such a sneaky little snake. How did you even get them to take you seriously without a parent with you?"

Eel blushed. "I got Alex to ring up Anna Popova pretending to be Gran and explain why she couldn't come with me."

Olivia gasped. "You are so deceitful. You should be so ashamed of yourself."

"Actually, Livy, I am," said Eel. She burst into tears. "It's all got a bit out of hand. Lying is such horribly hard work. I've hardly had time to concentrate on my dancing. It's all gone to pot, I've been so worried."

"Well, you'll have to turn the place down. You got it under false pretences."

"Actually, I got it because of my talent for ballet," said Eel.

"You're not going to try to go?" asked Olivia, shocked by Eel's brazenness. "It would break Gran's heart."

"I know," said Eel, and her eyes shone with tears. "I've realised that. In fact, I think I knew even when I was applying."

"Then how could you contemplate doing such a terrible thing? I don't understand."

Eel sighed. "Because I had to know whether I was good enough and Gran wouldn't tell me. I have to plan my future."

"For goodness' sake, Eel, you're nine!" snapped Olivia, exasperated. "You don't have to plan your future at nine."

"You do if you want to be a prima ballerina," said her sister, solemnly. "It's never too soon to start thinking about it. I'm already at a terrible disadvantage because I started ballet so late."

"But," said Olivia, "the Imperial must take

lots of girls every year and not all of them get to be ballerinas. Getting into the Imperial is no guarantee."

"I realise that," said Eel patiently. "But it is an indicator. I just wanted to know. And now I do, and I'm pleased I do. And providing you don't snitch, Gran and Dad need never know anything about it because I've decided to turn down the place. What they don't know need never upset them."

Olivia shook her head again. "Eel, it still feels so wrong," she said. "And aren't you worried that if you turn the Imperial down, they won't take you seriously if you apply again in the future?"

"I think they'll always take talent seriously," said Eel, without batting an eyelid. "All this has really made me think hard about what it is I want to do. I love ballet, but I love all types of dancing. I couldn't give any of them up, and that means the Swan is the best place for me. In fact, the only place."

"So all that deception and sneaking around was for nothing?" said Olivia.

"No," said Eel. "It was very useful. It made me realise that my desire to be at the Swan was stronger than my desire to be a ballerina." She paused. "And it made me realise that a life of crime would be completely and utterly exhausting."

The door of the bedroom slowly opened. Alicia stood on the threshold, leaning heavily on her stick. Her face was very serious.

"Eel," she said grimly. "I think you might have something you want to tell me."

Chapter Thirty-Eight

Eel was perched on Alicia's lap and Olivia was sitting at her feet. They'd been talking for over an hour. Eel had poured out everything that happened, although she had only finally admitted the role Alex had played under Alicia's constant questioning. Alicia had pursed her lips with displeasure and her eyes had flashed so dangerously that Eel felt as if all her insides had shrivelled away to nothing.

At one point, Alicia had actually shouted at her in disbelief and outrage, something which was unheard of for Alicia, who was always controlled, even in a crisis. Eel had shrunk away from her grandmother's disapproval. But the worst of the storm had passed, even though Alicia was still having her say.

244

"You do understand that what you've done is very serious, Eel? It's deception," she said.

Eel nodded; her eyes were red from crying and she was unusually subdued. "I know, Gran. I realised that very early on. But it was like pushing a boulder down a hill; once I had set it in motion, I couldn't stop it."

Alicia shook her head. "Maybe I'm to blame in part. If I had only let you audition in the first place, none of this would have happened. Perhaps I should have realised that you really needed to know and that nothing would stop you trying to find out."

"You shouldn't blame yourself, Gran. It's all my fault," said Eel.

"And you are quite certain you don't want to take up the place?" asked Alicia, quietly.

"I know what I want," said Eel, lifting her chin in determination. "I want to stay at the Swan."

"Then we must let Anna Popova know as soon as possible so that she can offer the place to another child."

"I want to go and see her and explain properly," said Eel.

Alicia smiled. "Well, you've got some

gumption, Eel, I'll give you that. And I'm proud of you for wanting to do the right thing."

When their grandmother left the room to make some hot chocolate for them all, Eel turned to her sister.

"Livy," said Eel. "There's something else I feel bad about."

Olivia raised an eyebrow. What other nefarious activities had Eel been up to?

"Go on, then, spit it out," she said. "It can't be any worse than what you've already confessed."

"It's just that I think I might have been the source of the story that was in the *Comet* about Jack being sick and about to quit."

"Why?" asked Olivia, curiously.

"It's just I told Alex Parks, but when I confronted him about it, he denied everything. I still feel really guilty about it, though. I shouldn't have blabbed like that."

Olivia wrinkled her nose. "I'm not Alex Parks' biggest fan, as you know, but I very much doubt that he's a spy for the Viktor camp. Listen, Eel, don't beat yourself up about it. All of us let things slip in conversation. It's hard to keep a secret. Even Aeysha told her mum about the fireworks. Have you told him anything else?"

Eel shook her head. "No, I've been giving him a wide berth."

"There you are, then," said Olivia. "Loads of stuff has been coming out and you haven't said a word. And it can't be Alex, either. None of us are that close to him."

Chapter Thirty-Nine

It was very early in the morning before school. The wind was vicious. Olivia and Tom were down at the river, watching Jack. The Great Marvello was crouched on the wire, gazing moodily into the dark water below.

"He won't be broken," said Pablo. "I've asked him again and again if he wants to call it a day, but he refuses to give up."

"You don't think he should, do you?" asked Olivia, sharply.

"Of course not," said Pablo. "But I want to give him the choice. I don't want him to feel that he has to go on when there's no..." Pablo tailed off miserably.

"No point," said Olivia, furiously.

"I didn't mean that, Livy," said Pablo. "But

the situation is pretty hopeless." He waved a hand around. "Half the team has quit. There's very little support. People just come and stand on the bridge and shout abuse. It must be awful for Jack to deal with it hour after hour, day after day. I worry about what it's doing to him."

"Any news from Viktor's camp?" asked Tom.

"Only that Viktor is on his last legs. Still, he's only got to last out another couple of days and he'll have won. Even if Jack stays up there to the end, no one believes he hasn't cheated."

"It's so unfair!" said Olivia, fiercely.

"You haven't managed to find anything out?" asked Pablo.

Olivia shook her head. "But we've not given up. We won't. Not ever."

Tom and Pablo glanced at each other. They knew Olivia would never rest until she had cleared Jack's name.

Alex was up on the roof of the Swan, talking on his phone.

"Please, Dad, don't make me do this. I want out. I only said yes in the first place because I wanted to get my own back on Olivia Marvell, and I thought it would help you get a job on that American tour that Ethan Rees is organising. I never realised I'd be involved in wrecking a man's entire reputation. I feel like a complete rat."

"Look, Alex," wheedled his dad, "this is my one big chance. Don't spoil it for me. Or your mum. You know how much it would mean to her."

Alex's heart contracted at the mention of his mum, so patient and uncomplaining despite the constant pain she was in.

"But things have changed, Dad. I feel differently now. I don't bear Olivia Marvell any ill will. In fact, I rather admire her dad for sticking it out in the face of so much adversity. And I certainly don't want to compromise Georgia in any way."

"It's a bit too late to get a conscience, Alex. What's done is done." His dad sighed. "Alex. Please. All I need is one more bit of info to put Ethan Rees forever in my debt and I'll be a dead cert on his next US tour. Think of your mum."

It was lunchtime, and Olivia, Aeysha and Tom were in the dining hall. Georgia was nowhere to be seen. Aeysha looked around the room. Alex was missing, too. She guessed that they were both off somewhere together.

Tom was watching Olivia picking at her food. She'd hardly eaten a thing. "Liv, you've done everything you could to try to prove your dad's innocence," he said, quietly.

"I've done my best but my best hasn't been good enough," said Olivia, wanly. "I've failed him."

"You're not to blame," said Aeysha. "Don't beat yourself up about it."

"That's exactly what I said to Eel yesterday," said Olivia. "She got it into her head that she was to blame for that *Comet* piece about Jack's health that came out right at the start of the stunt. She was really letting it eat her up."

"Why'd she think that?" asked Aeysha.

Olivia gave a mirthless little laugh. "Apparently she told Alex Parks about Dad not being in great shape. Even if she did, that leak could have come from anywhere, and she's had nothing to do with him since. None of us have really had any contact with…" She broke off as she saw Aeysha and Tom staring at her in horror.

"What is it?" asked Olivia, urgently.

Her friends were looking at her as if the ceiling had just fallen in.

"Did you know?" said Aeysha, looking questioningly at Tom.

He nodded, embarrassed. "I just didn't think it was my business."

"What?" demanded Olivia. "What are you both talking about."

"Georgia," whispered Aeysha. "Oh poor, poor Georgia."

Chapter Forty

"I've spoken to Pablo, and he's game, so are we agreed?" asked Olivia. Tom and Aeysha nodded.

"But I feel rubbish about doing it," said Tom.

"I know," said Olivia. "It's a horrible thing to do to a friend, but I can't see any other way. Can you?" They shook their heads. "We haven't got enough evidence to confront him, and it will be even worse for our future friendship with Georgia if we go round making accusations and it turns out that we're completely wrong. Georgie would never forgive us."

"I'm not sure she's going to forgive us anyway," said Aeysha, quietly. "I want it to be true for Jack's sake because it will be one step closer to clearing his name. But even though I don't much like Alex Parks, the other part of me wants it all to be a horrible coincidence. I thought that he was using Georgia to get his own back on you, Olivia, but to think he was going out with her to pump her for information is creepy."

"But if that's the case and you were Georgia, wouldn't you want to know?" asked Olivia.

"Yes," said Aeysha, seriously, and tears flooded her eyes. "I would, but it wouldn't make it hurt any less."

"Of course there could be another possibility, an even worse one," said Tom, but he looked really embarrassed. "What if Alex isn't tricking her into giving him information? What if Georgia's colluding with him?"

The others looked at him, horrified.

"I didn't say I thought that was the case," said Tom hastily, seeing their faces. "I'm just saying it is a possibility."

"No," said Olivia, fiercely. "Georgia might blurt things out sometimes without thinking, but I'm not going to believe that she's in league with Alex any more than I'm prepared to believe that my dad is a cheat."

The others nodded.

"Well," said Aeysha. "I think Olivia's plan is a good one. At least this way Georgie will see Alex Parks for what he really is, if it does turn out that he's the source of the leaks."

"Yes," said Olivia. "But she might not thank us for opening her eyes."

It was lunchtime the following day. Olivia and Tom had just sat down with their trays when they saw Georgia in the food queue.

"Over here," waved Olivia, with a smile. Georgia came over and plonked herself down, Aeysha following not far behind. Olivia saw Georgia glance around the hall and take in the table where Alex was sitting talking to some Year Ten boys. He looked up as she looked his way, and for the briefest of moments it seemed to Olivia as if their eyes locked.

"How are things with Jack? Any better?" asked Georgia, chattily, as she put tomato ketchup on her fish fingers.

Olivia glanced at Aeysha. "Not good," replied Olivia.

"Oh Livy, I'm so sorry," said Georgia, putting her hand over Olivia's. "I just wish we'd been able to prove that he's the victim of a dirty tricks campaign by Viktor." She shook her head as if she couldn't believe that anybody could behave so appallingly.

"Me, too," said Olivia. She took a deep breath. It was now or never. "Actually, Georgie, Jack's in quite bad shape. Pablo's really worried about him. He's arranged for a doctor to come down and see him at five o'clock this evening. Jack doesn't know. We're all going down to be there. I think he's going to need all the support he can get because Pablo is certain that the doctor will call a halt on medical grounds. I want to be there when it's all over."

"I'll come," said Georgia. "I was supposed to meet someone, but I want to be there to show my support when Jack comes off the wire for the very last time."

"Thanks, Georgia," said Olivia. "That's really nice of you."

She felt like a complete rat. She just hoped that Georgia would be able to find it in her heart to forgive her.

"Hi, babe."

"Alex, it's Georgia."

256

"I know," Alex laughed. "Your name comes up on my screen. I don't go round calling everyone who rings me 'babe'."

"Sorry!" said Georgia. "How silly."

"It's not silly, it's sweet."

"Alex, I can't meet you at five. Sorry it's such late notice but I haven't had a chance to call before."

"Oh. That's a shame."

Georgia could hear the disappointment in his voice. "I wouldn't blow you out but it's important. I'm going down to the river with Livy and the others. Pablo's called a doctor in. They're going to get Jack off the wire. It's the end. I have to go. Livy will be in a terrible state and I want to be there for my friend."

"I understand," said Alex softly. Then he added: "You're such a nice person, Georgia. I don't deserve you."

"You're nice, too, Alex," said Georgia. "One day my friends will realise that."

Alex cringed. How he longed to tell her the truth! But he couldn't. It would destroy her and it would destroy his dad. He couldn't do it to either of them. How he wished he could turn back the clock to the day he'd said he'd help to bring Jack Marvell down. He had been consumed with fury at Olivia and on the spur of the moment had done something that had already destroyed one person's reputation, and might yet destroy others.

They said goodbye. Alex stood still for a moment. So Jack Marvell was going to be defeated. He felt sorry for the man. But he felt sorry for his dad, too. Ethan Rees had made so many promises. He'd said he would look after the family. He would get Alex's mum the best treatment possible. He'd move them all to the States. Alex wasn't at all sure that Rees could be believed, but his dad clung to every word. He begged Alex to help him and Alex couldn't bear to see his desperate face.

Anyway, what did it matter now what he did? Nothing could hasten the end, that was a foregone conclusion. Passing this final snippet of information on would surely be enough to keep a struggling Viktor going and ensure that Alex's dad earned Rees' eternal devotion.

Alex pressed a number on his phone. He was doing this for the very last time. He felt terrible about it, but he comforted himself with the fact that it would have no impact on Jack

Marvell. He was already a beaten man.

* * *

Olivia and the others were huddled together by the edge of the river, stamping their feet to try and keep out the cold. They had all linked arms in an effort to stay warm, but Georgia had made a point of standing between Tom and Olivia. Things between her and Aeysha were still tense.

"We're like penguins," observed Tom, trying to lighten the mood. The wind was whipping their hair and it seemed to be trying to snow again. The area was deserted. The crowds had long given up baiting Jack and even the media had lost interest in its fallen hero.

It was a quarter to five. Olivia looked anxiously around. She didn't know what she wanted. If the press and media came, it would prove that Alex Parks was the mole. But if they didn't, it could mean one of two things: either Georgia hadn't passed the information on, or Olivia and the others had been quite wrong to suspect that Alex was involved. For her friend's sake, Olivia hoped that it was the latter. She saw Aeysha biting her lip and looking around with a frown on her face. It was increasingly beginning to look as if they had been mistaken. Surely the press ought to be swarming all over the place by now?

Suddenly, from a distance, they heard the sound of a speedboat racing up the river, and at the same time there was a screech of tyres as a car stopped and behind it came the roar of a motor bike.

Within seconds, the riverbank was swarming with reporters and photographers. The speedboat they'd heard was circling under the wire so that the photographers aboard could get a better view. A TV crew arrived and a crowd of interested people was gathering on the bridge, drawn by all the activity. A few of them booed Jack, who simply ignored them. The reporters crowded around Pablo, who climbed on to a wooden box so that he could be seen better. Two TV reporters thrust microphones under his nose.

"So, when will the doctor be here to certify that it would be unsafe for Jack Marvell to continue?"

"Is it true that he is having both a mental and physical breakdown?"

"Will he be taken to hospital?"

"Is he a broken man?"

Pablo smiled. "I don't know where you got your information from, but I'm afraid you're quite mistaken. There's no doctor coming and Jack Marvell is definitely not a broken man. Broken men don't do things like that."

He pointed behind them and all the reporters turned to see Jack flipping along the wire in a dizzying display of acrobatics so astonishing that some of the press broke into applause.

"What's going on?" asked Georgia, confused. "Where's the doctor? I don't understand."

"Georgie," said Tom gently, "did you tell anyone about the doctor coming down to the river tonight and about Jack throwing in the towel?"

"Of course not," said Georgia, furiously. "What do you think I am, some kind of spy..." She choked on the word "spy" and turned ghost-white.

"Georgia," said Olivia. "This is really important. Who did you tell what was going to happen this afternoon?"

Georgia bowed her head. "Alex," she whispered in a broken voice. "I told Alex Parks."

"Oh, Georgie, I'm so sorry," said Olivia. "It seems that Alex Parks can't be trusted. I don't know how or why, but he must have been feeding information about Jack to Viktor. We think he might even be involved in some way in the fake video."

Georgia stared at her. "So," she whispered. "This whole thing was a set-up to trick me."

"No," said Olivia, desperately. "Nobody wanted to trick you. Nobody suspected you of doing anything wrong. We just needed to know if our suspicions about Alex were right."

Georgia glared at her and then at Aeysha. Her face was desperate. "What a horrible, *horrible* thing to do to a friend," she said. "And it doesn't prove anything. It could have been any one of you. It's not Alex, I know it's not, I'd swear on my life…"

A shout came from the towpath. It was Kasha. "Livy! I've found something out." He raced towards the Swans.

The reporters who had been watching Jack suddenly realised who the newcomer was. They crowded round Kasha, who was so eager to give Olivia and the others his news that he ploughed on anyway, not noticing their stricken faces.

"I went back to the hotel and spoke to Tilda Soames again. Or Matty, as her family call her. I got her talking about her family, in fact. They've got showbiz connections. She's the half-sister of a guy called Andy Parks, an impressionist. I had a poke around and discovered that he's worked with Rees in the past, he toured America with him. Then I remembered Livy mentioning there was an Alex Parks at the Swan. I checked it out. He's his son."

Georgia gave a sob and buried her face in her hands.

"But there's more," said Kasha, oblivious to Georgia's distress. "Look!" He held up his phone and showed them a small clip. "This is Andy Parks impersonating Jack during a show. It's taken about the same time Jack had that plane crash in Idaho."

"So," said Olivia. "It could have been Andy Parks checking into the hotel in the videos, pretending to be Dad?"

Some of the reporters, who'd been listening to all this with great interest, were busy shouting into their phones, asking their researchers to find out whatever they could on Andy Parks, and the rest were crowding around Kasha, firing questions at him. There was so much noise that it took a second or two for the others to realise that Georgia had detached herself from the group and was running along the towpath in the direction of the Swan.

"I'll go after her," said Aeysha. "You stay here and see how things develop."

She set off at a sprint, but Georgia was flying like the wind.

Georgia raced into the Swan and halted. Some of the older students, who'd stayed late at school to start rehearsing their end-of-year showcase, were standing in a gaggle in the hall.

She heard one of them say: "Hey guys, look at this on Twitter. It seems Jack Marvell could be innocent after all. Apparently someone's been playing dirty tricks."

Another one whistled. "Shall we go down to the river and see what's going on?"

Georgia slipped into the girls' changing room and waited until they had left the building, laughing and joking as they went. Then she raced downstairs to one of the music rooms and slammed the door behind her.

Aeysha arrived at the Swan just a few

minutes later. She hadn't known that Georgia could run so fast. Just as she started up the steps she heard wild footsteps behind her. She swung round. As soon as she saw Alex's face, she knew that he knew.

"Where's Georgia? I've got to talk to her," he said desperately. "I've tried ringing and texting her but she's not answering. I need to talk to her."

"To do what?" asked Aeysha. "To explain that you betrayed her and Jack? What was your price, Alex? Thirty pieces of silver?"

Alex flinched as if she had physically hit him. "I don't want to make excuses, Aeysha. There are no excuses for what I've done. I just want to see her one last time, to tell her how sorry I am."

There was something about his abject misery that touched Aeysha. "OK," she said. "I shouldn't trust you, but I do. I expect you'll find her in the music room. Number three. It's where she often goes when she's down. But I'll be right outside, and if you do anything more to hurt her, Alex Parks, I'll track you down to the very ends of the earth."

Chapter Forty-One

Alex slowly pushed open the door of the music room. He took a deep breath and stepped inside.

"Georgie?" he whispered.

Georgia was sitting hunched on the piano stool with her knees drawn up. She glanced at him. His striking face was pale; his eyes troubled. She shifted so her back was turned to him and shuffled closer towards the piano so her head was resting on the closed lid. It was as if she was trying to get as far away from him as possible.

"Go away," she said in a cold, hard voice.

"Georgia," he pleaded. "Let me just talk to you, please let me explain."

Georgia lifted her head, her eyes blazing. "Explain? What is there to explain? Everything is crystal clear to me and to everybody else. You used me. You used me so you and your dad could get at Jack Marvell. I was an idiot ever to fall for it. Go away and leave me alone."

Alex turned back towards the door. But then he stopped. "Georgie, I can't leave you like this. I know I've hurt you. I know you won't ever be able to forgive me for what I did. But I want you to know the truth."

"Truth!" spat Georgia. "It doesn't seem to be one of your strengths. You deceived us all and lied to me. You made me think that it was me, little Georgia Jones, that you were interested in. But it was all just a lie to find out information so you could discredit Livy's dad and get your revenge on Livy. You're despicable, Alex Parks, a sewer rat has more morals than you."

Alex shook his head sadly. "You're right, Georgia, what I did was awful and I am truly sorry. I really am. But you've got to believe me when I tell you that I never set out to hurt you."

"Oh, don't think that you have, Alex Parks. I wouldn't give you the satisfaction," said Georgia. Her voice was trembling and her eyes shone with fury.

"Georgia," Alex said, urgently, "I had to do it. My dad was desperate. He hasn't worked for months. My mum's sick. Our family was falling apart. When I told Dad that Olivia Marvell and her sister were here at the Swan, he saw a way to make an easy buck. It wasn't all planned out. It was just opportunism. He asked me to feed him what information I could so that he could be useful to Ethan Rees. At first I said no, but when Livy humiliated me, I decided to do what I could for him."

"Like a spy," snarled Georgia.

Alex nodded miserably. "I swear it wasn't like that at first. He just seemed really interested in Livy and her dad and his stunt down by the river. It was only later that he started putting pressure on me to find out as much as I could."

"So," asked Georgia, slowly. "When you first came to the Swan and you tried to get closer to Livy, were you just pretending you liked her, or did you really like her?"

Alex shuffled his feet. He hesitated, and then he said: "I thought she was gorgeous. I genuinely wanted to get to know her better. I'd never met a girl quite like her. Most girls fall at my feet."

Georgia took a deep breath. "And me? When Livy gave you the brush-off and you turned your attention to me, was that real or were you faking?"

There was a tiny, charged silence and then Alex looked Georgia straight in the eye. "I can't lie, Georgia. At first, getting close to you was just a ploy. A way of getting back at Livy and helping my dad at the same time."

"And I made it easy for you," said Georgia, bitterly. "I just swooned at your feet."

"No! Yes … er, no. Listen! Please, please listen. That's what I need to explain. Georgie, at first I was just trying to get info from you to help my dad. I thought we'd have some fun together, then when I'd got all the info my dad needed, we'd just break up. No hard feelings. But after the first couple of weeks, it wasn't like that at all. It got more complicated. You're a such lovely girl, Georgie. You don't know how many of the boys really like you. And I … I… Georgia, I really fell for you. I wasn't pretending, I promise. And I thought you felt the same."

Georgia's heart gave a lurch, but she couldn't bear the thought of making herself vulnerable to him again. She gave a hollow little laugh. "You're a self-confessed liar," she said. "Why should I believe a word you say?"

"Because it's true," said Alex, softly.

"Then go down to the river and confess. In front of the press. Then tell Jack you're sorry," said Georgia.

Alex look scared. "It's too much to ask, Georgie."

"Then leave me alone, Alex. You've already done enough damage."

"I know. I'm so, so sorry."

He turned and left the studio, his shoulders hunched and his entire body engulfed in misery. Georgia put her head against the piano lid, and cried and cried. After a while the door opened again and Aeysha walked quietly into the room. She said nothing, but slid on to the edge of the piano stool next to Georgia, put her arms around her and held her very tight.

Chapter Forty-Two

The wind whistled around the bridge, blowing the snowflakes into a blizzard that made them look as if they were fighting each other. Most of the city was silent, wrapped in an icy cocoon. But down at Tower Bridge, a full media circus had set up camp. The reporters had been digging around and they'd come up with plenty of evidence of connections between the Parks family and Ethan Rees, but nothing yet that categorically proved Andy Parks had been impersonating Jack in the incriminating videos.

Jack was in good spirits, having been briefed by Olivia and Pablo when he had taken a break from the wire, but he was keeping his mouth shut until more evidence had been found.

He didn't want to make any rash statements or say anything that could be construed as crowing. Eventually, he'd retreated to his hammock for half an hour to get away from the constant glare of the cameras.

"But what if no solid evidence is found?" asked Olivia, anxiously. She was feeling low. After the excitement of the late afternoon when she had thought that Jack's innocence was about to be proved beyond all doubt, she was upset by the lack of an instant happy conclusion.

She was also worried about Georgia. Aeysha had texted to say that she'd taken her back to her house, but she wondered whether the group could ever be the same. It felt as if something had been irrevocably broken.

Olivia walked moodily down towards the water, kicking a stone and oblivious to the snow that was settling across her head and shoulders.

"Liv!" She swung round. Alex was standing on the towpath. What could he want with her? Olivia walked up towards him. When she got near he looked smaller than she remembered. His face was pale and his cheeks hollow. He looked like a living statue. The snow was settling on his hair and eyelashes so it was as if somebody had sprinkled him with tiny glittering stars.

"What do you want?" she asked warily.

For a moment, Alex said nothing, as if he had something caught in his throat and he couldn't speak.

"I want to tell Jack I'm sorry," he whispered.

Olivia felt the fury rise in her throat, but Alex was such a picture of misery that it died as quickly as it had sparked. "And I want to give you this," he said, thrusting his phone into her hand. "Look at the messages," he said.

He walked away from her down towards the river. Olivia looked down at the phone in her hand and clicked through the messages. Here it all was, all the evidence that was needed to prove Andy Parks' involvement with Rees and Viktor and their attempts to scupper Jack's world-record attempt. There were even some emails from Ethan Rees to Alex's dad, detailing the kind of intelligence that would be helpful and which Andy Parks had forwarded to his son.

Alex had given her everything that she needed to prove Jack's innocence. With a noise that was half a cry of triumph and half a sob, she ran towards Pablo.

"It's here," she shouted. "All the evidence is here!"

She thrust the phone into his hand and immediately they were surrounded by a gaggle of journalists. Suddenly, a great shout went up from the people on the bridge. She wondered whether Jack had emerged from the hammock. Pablo was still excitedly talking to the journalists, but Olivia pushed her way out from their midst to see what was happening. What she saw made her heart thump.

Alex was up on the wire, edging precariously along it towards the middle where Jack's hammock swung. Olivia put her hand to her mouth and began running towards the water. What had Alex said? *I want to tell Jack I'm sorry.* But she had never imagined that he meant to do it straight away.

Alex took another wobbly step. To her horror, Olivia realised that he wasn't wearing a safety harness. He wouldn't last more than a few seconds on the wire in these conditions. He didn't have either the skill or the experience to deal with the dangers. Another few steps and he would feel the full force of the wind, which would play with him until it knocked him off his perch into the icy dark waters below.

Olivia didn't hesitate. There was only one spare safety harness, and it was hanging at the end of the wire. She grabbed it, slung it over her shoulder and stepped out on to the wire after Alex. She heard Pablo shout "No!" behind her. She saw Jack stick his head out of the hammock and a look of horror cross his face as he saw both her and Alex on the wire.

"Don't move," Olivia warned Jack. She knew that if Jack tried to clamber on to the wire, it would sway and tip Alex into the water. She wasn't even sure that she would survive the vibrations, either. She glanced down at where the river lay in wait like a hungry monster.

Jack instantly saw the danger and stayed as still as a statute, his eyes fixed on the children as if willing them to stay upright. The snow continued to fall silently around them. It felt as if everyone watching from the bridge and the banks of the river was holding their breath, too.

Several boats were circling under the wire, their engines turned down low. Olivia was beginning to gain on Alex. She was trying to step as lightly as she could to avoid setting up vibrations in the wire. If she could just get to

Alex and slip the safety harness around him and clip it to the wire, it wouldn't matter if he fell.

Now the snow was falling in great clots, so it was hard to see more than a few steps ahead and the wire was becoming treacherous. A sudden gust of wind felt like a punch in the stomach and made Olivia gasp. But she didn't falter. She saw Alex teeter and held her breath, thinking that he would certainly fall. In the nick of time, he recovered his balance. But he looked so fragile, as if another gust could catch him and pitch him off the wire at any moment.

"It's Alex, isn't it? Just stay where you are, son," called Jack, softly. He thought he recognised the boy as a Swan. He also thought he'd never seen anyone look so terrified.

"But I need to talk to you, Mr Marvell. I need to tell you that I'm sorry for everything."

"I'm sure you don't have anything to be sorry about, Alex, but let's talk about it on firm ground. Please just stay where you are. Someone is coming to get you. They've got a safety harness. They're going to help you."

Alex tried to turn to look behind him and he swayed back and forth like a piece of washing badly pegged to a line.

"Don't move and keep talking to me," said Jack, desperately. If he could only keep the boy still, perhaps Olivia would get to him in time. Jack was scared for him, but more scared that, if he fell, he would cause the wire to sway so much that Olivia would plummet into the river, too.

"I didn't mean for all these people to get hurt," shouted Alex. "But Ethan Rees offered my dad a job in America and money if he would make the videos. He was desperate, you see. But I never thought that it would destroy you so completely ... I've been such a..."

The journalists in the boat below were straining to hear and scribbling furiously.

"Alex, it's all right," said Jack soothingly. "Don't upset yourself." He looked anxiously at Olivia who had almost reached Alex. She glanced at her dad.

"Alex," he said urgently, "you must try to raise your arms. Be very gentle so you don't lose your balance, and Liv will slip the safety harness over you."

"Livy!?" Alex tried to swing round. He looked at Olivia with astonishment. "After everything I've done to destroy you and your

277

family, you came out on the wire to save me." His eyes were full of tears, his face a mask of pain.

Olivia reached out to try and steady him, their hands brushed, and then Alex plunged off the wire into the swirling water below and was swallowed up.

Further along the river, Viktor Ivanov crawled out of his hammock and hauled himself on to the wire. From the riverbank, the tiny figure walking towards the shore looked about a hundred years old. He reached the end of the wire and started to clamber down.

Ethan Rees ran towards him. "Viktor! Viktor, my boy, what are you doing? It's not one of your scheduled breaks. Get back on that wire at once! We're not done yet."

Viktor ignored him and started trudging towards the path. "I am," he said, very quietly. "I'm finished. It's over."

"Come back!" yelled Ethan Rees. "There are only two days to go. You can still win."

But Viktor just kept on walking, and as he did so, Rees's phone began to chirp with messages, and suddenly a posse of journalists appeared and began running towards him, shouting about videos, fraud and deception. The slight figure walking along the towpath didn't even look back.

Chapter Forty-Three

Tom and Katie were anxiously scanning the crowds pouring into the foyer of the venue. Katie was back from Yorkshire after filming her part in the TV series. Alicia and Jack were standing nearby, and several people were crowded around Jack, asking for his autograph and wanting their photograph taken with him. Others shouted out their good wishes, and a man was clapping Jack on the back, congratulating him on breaking the world record and saying they needed more heroes like him.

"That's not what people were saying a week ago," muttered Katie, dryly.

Tom was still looking around. "You don't think Liv and Georgia have got lost?"

"No, look! There they are," said Katie.

Olivia and Georgia were coming towards them with their arms linked.

"Are you both all right?" asked Tom, scanning their faces anxiously.

"Yes," said Georgia. "I'm glad we went to the hospital to see Alex. It felt like..." She searched for the right word. "It felt right."

"How is he?" asked Katie.

"Well, apart from a collapsed lung and the fact that he swallowed half of the Thames, reasonably OK," said Olivia. "It was just lucky all those boats were there to pick him up so quickly or he probably would have drowned."

"He's different," said Georgia, quietly. "Nicer. It's a better way to remember him."

"He won't be coming back to the Swan then?"

Olivia shook her head. "I don't think it was ever an option. His dad's facing a police investigation but, when that's over, Alex says they're going to move out of London."

"But he said he'd write to me," added Georgia.

Katie frowned.

"Don't you frown at me," said Georgia. "I'm so over Alex Parks. I don't know what I ever saw in him."

"Good looks? Oodles of charm?" said Katie, with a grin.

"Nah," said Georgia, with a wicked smile. "That's not my type."

She linked arms with Katie and they strolled over to look at the merchandise.

Tom and Olivia watched them go.

"Do you think Georgia's really OK?" he asked Olivia.

"Well, she's putting a brave face on it. Of course she's bruised, but Aeysha's been amazing with her. They've talked a lot, and after we'd been to the hospital she said that although she was furious at the time, she realised that we were just trying to protect her when we laid the plan to trap Alex."

"It was probably good that we've all been so busy this week with *Dream* rehearsals. The performance went well this afternoon, didn't it?" said Tom.

"Yes, it was lovely," agreed Olivia, "although I can't wear my costume without thinking of Kasha hobbling out of that hotel in it. He makes such a lovely girl."

"You'd better not tell Lucie Groves. She'd

have a fit."

"She won't stop asking him how he got out of the hotel, but he just says that he sprouted wings and flew," said Olivia, with a grin. "Which reminds me, where are Imy and Gem?"

At that moment, they appeared. Olivia greeted them enthusiastically. "Tom," she said, "this is Imy and Gem. They are Kasha's number one fans, and he's really looking forward to meeting them after the show." She handed the two girls their tickets for the concert, back-stage passes and invites to the after-show party.

Imy and Gem squealed. "I won't know what to say to him!" said Imy.

"Oh," said Olivia, with a wicked smile. "If you're stuck for words, why don't you ask Kasha about my Aunt Belinda. He's very, very fond of her. I don't know what he sees in her myself."

At that moment, Eel came waltzing up with Emmy and Esme, who'd come down from Yorkshire to stay for the weekend.

"Liv! This is my friend, Esme." Eel was looking at Esme proudly. "Esme is going to the Imperial. She's a fantastic dancer."

Olivia smiled at the little girl. "You must be

very good," she said.

"Eel's as good, maybe better," said Esme, generously.

"No, I'm not," said Eel. "You're the one who got the scholarship."

"Only after another girl gave it up," said her friend. She shook her head. "I don't know how anyone could think of giving up a scholarship to the Imperial."

Eel looked at Olivia and the two sisters exchanged little smiles.

Alicia came over and touched Olivia's shoulder. "We must take our seats. Kasha's about to come on stage."

The final note of "Bruised" faded away. There was a tiny electrified silence and then the sell-out crowd began whooping and stamping their approval of the acoustic duet that Kasha and Aeysha had just sung. Aeysha looked very tiny and rather dazed, but she was beaming broadly as the audience clapped and cheered.

"Ladies and gentlemen," said Kasha, with a big smile. "I give you my songwriting partner, Aeysha Aziz, without whom I'd never have written the number-one hit, 'Bruised'. Aeysha."

Aeysha bowed and the crowd roared their approval. Olivia and the others were on their feet, cheering and stamping. Eel was hopping from foot to foot in her excitement. Georgia was shouting Aeysha's name over and over again, Tom had his hands raised right over his head and Katie was screaming her delight.

Olivia looked from Aeysha's glowing face to those of her excited friends and listened to their happy, generous applause. She caught Georgia's eye and Georgia smiled at her, a gentle, forgiving smile. They had all come through so much together in the last few weeks, they had had some narrow escapes but they had emerged bruised but unbroken.

Suddenly, it occurred to Olivia. "We're growing up," she said, out loud.

There was wonder in her voice, but nobody else heard it because there was too much noise. She looked at her friends' shining faces.

"Growing up," she whispered to herself, "but not growing apart."